The Summers We Left Behind

Copyright © 2023 by Marja Graham

All rights reserved.

No part of this publication may be reproduced, distributed, or transmitted in any form or by any means, including photocopying, recording, or other electronic or mechanical methods, without the prior written permission of the publisher, except as permitted by U.S. copyright law. For permission requests, contact the author.

The story, all names, characters, and incidents portrayed in this production are fictitious. No identification with actual persons (living or deceased), places, buildings, and products is intended or should be inferred.

Book Cover by Grace Steffen. Instagram gracesteffenart

To anyone who has dreamed of summer boys and first loves.
And to Stef, without you these all would be blank pages.

1
Saturday
Now

There's an angry ocean in my stomach threatening to make itself known.

The car jostles, waking me from a hazy sleep as we run through a sea of potholes. The problem is I don't remember getting into the car, where I'm now wedged into the backseat. I look up, blinking the sleep from my eyes, and make out a minivan full of people. Upon a brief inspection, my kidnappers are my friends.

Who do I know that looks like they drive a minivan? How did I end up in the backseat of said minivan with a raging hangover? And most importantly, where are we going?

I realize the only reason I don't hear everyone singing along to the music is that I have a pair of headphones on blocking it out. I lift one earbud, but the onslaught of sound overloads my fragile senses, and I replace it.

Yesterday, I had the most picture-perfect boyfriend and a relaxing week ahead of me. Today, neither of those things that I took as facts are true. Jackson and I had been planning on spending spring break at his parent's cabin in the Smoky

Mountains. It would have been us, endless miles of trails, and a very secluded hot tub.

I was happy that he wasn't insisting on some large group getaway to a resort, like he did last year. I hadn't known most of the people in the group, and I had taken the unlimited drink package as a challenge. The smell of coconut rum still makes me gag.

Perfect plans like that change when you find your partner in bed with another girl the night before you're supposed to leave. What makes it worse is that he didn't even try to fix it. In every TV show, movie, or book, the guy chases after you, leaves endless text messages, or even begs your best friend to give him one last shot. He didn't even give me the satisfaction of needing to block his number or tell him to fuck off.

No, Jackson just looked me in the eyes while wrapped up in his damn cliché navy sheets and said, "Oh shit."

Two entire years, and we weren't worth fighting for. I wasn't worth fighting for. I wasn't even worth a hasty and poorly written text. I think that girl stayed with him long after I left. He might have even offered her my spot on the trip. He's probably charming her into the hot tub right now.

Time became very liquid after that incident. I called up Libby, who was ready to drown my tears in alcohol the moment she heard the words 'breakup' and 'cheater.' She brought my comfort take-out order and a selection of the smallest shirts I've ever seen.

"If he can't appreciate you, these will help you find other people who do," She had said, holding up a scrap of sequins.

I ate my Pad Thai while I was given a lecture on why Jackson was the worst boyfriend ever and an overall vile human being. She had pointed out everything he'd done over the years and how it was his loss, not mine.

"I never told you, but that first year you were dating, he had to text me asking when your birthdays was at least five times. Also, remember how he called from the bar asking you to pick him up when the only reason you didn't join was because you had an exam in the morning? He was so self-centered."

Was I blind to all the small things that should have added up to a failed relationship? Or were they just the little things hiding our relationship's larger flaws? We never had an explosive type of love, but over the last semester, what we did have started to fizzle out. It began to feel more and more like we were only together because it felt like what we were supposed to do.

Last night, I wanted to stay in, inhale a bottle of wine, and watch trashy reality TV. The type where the celebrities' heinous lives make you feel better by comparison. That was until Libby pulled the senior year of college card.

We only have two months left at Haven University, and the countdown is feeling too real.

We pull the senior year card anytime someone needed a final reason to do something big. It's why Libby shaved her head, which she now dyes with intricate patterns. From my seat in the car, I can see the vibrant red and orange flames peeking out from the passenger seat.

It's also how we finally convinced Caleb to get the tattoo of a cow he'd been incessantly talking about for three years. I was about to give it to him myself if I had to hear about the pet cow he helped deliver, and that eventually became his best friend growing up, one more time. Don't get me wrong, it's a cute story, but hearing about the miracles of cow birth seventeen times can become anyone's villain origin story.

And it worked well enough for me to tie on a top that was barely a piece of fabric and paint on mascara.

When I think back hard enough, my brain starts to short-circuit. Fragments of memories come back to me. I remember the flashing lights from our favorite bar, Stairway to Haven, and an endless stream of tequila shots. It's our favorite bar partly because of the back room, affectionately called Hell's Gate, where there is nothing but gyrating bodies and eardrum shattering music. And partly because ordering a single at Stairway to Haven is more like a double, and a double is just straight liquor.

I also remember that strangers were very eager to help me use alcohol as a bandage to mend my pride or, rather, make me forget my pride altogether.

I have left little pride after last night if the snapshots of my swan dive off a barstool are accurate. The patchwork of bruises on my arms is enough evidence to think I had fallen more than once throughout the night.

Where did I sleep?

If the credit card notifications on my phone are any indicator, I didn't make it home until after two in the morning. They also paint a nightmarish picture of how much damage I've done to my bank account. The timeline doesn't leave much room for sleeping, packing, and driving.

I don't remember curling up in my bed, and my face is still crusted with last night's makeup. As someone who does her skincare more religiously while drunk than sober, this is not the best sign.

At some point, I must have gone home because I'm wearing my own oversized t-shirt and sweatpants. There's a stuffed duffle by my feet, but I hope whoever dragged me into this car was responsible for cramming it full of my belongings. If I packed it, my guess would be that it's filled with fifteen pairs of underwear, a swimsuit, and maybe toothpaste.

In my lap is the stockpile of the motion sickness medication I keep on hand, my phone, and a neon yellow sports drink. These explain why I haven't spilled the contents of my stomach over the car, though I do remember leaning over a toilet last night. The medication also must be why my head feels like the jackhammer buzzing in my head has only been set on low.

The view outside is a blur of lush green. The air is touched with salt. The word 'beach' might have been passed around last night.

That sounds about right.

Most students at Haven end up somewhere on the coast for the break. My freshman year roommate, Beth, went to Miami and returned with one of the ten pairs of underwear she'd packed. I never asked where they went—I didn't want to know.

I'd look outside to see if there are any signs indicating what state we're in but looking at the world zipping by will only send my head spinning violently.

I allow myself to tumble back into the abyss of sleep, hoping it will help revive me before being thrown into whatever plans the other van occupants have in store for the rest of the day.

"Hey, Emma." A shoulder nudges me back to consciousness. I assume we're almost there. Wherever *there* is.

"Ummm," I grumble. "What." The words come out rough. My tongue is tacky, sticking to the roof of my mouth.

God, I need water.

"She's alive!" Libby and Jess yell. I recoil. Their cheers are like a buzzer going off in my brain.

"You said last night that you lived around here. Where is the best place to stop to grab groceries for the week?" Caleb asks from the front seat. I'm guessing the van is his, now that I see the cowboy hat shaped air freshener hanging from the rearview mirror.

Why would he be asking that? I'm from D.C. I've lived there my entire life. So, unless the city had replaced its national monuments and tourist packed sidewalks with a forest of trees, I have no idea where we are.

Out the window, a sign flashes by 'Harriettesville 5 Miles.' Then it hits me.

Shit.

I'm not counting the four summers my family spent in Harriettesville, North Carolina. I haven't talked about the beach house and those summers since before college. Well, unless I'm in therapy. My new life at Haven is a shield I've used to block out those years. It is a testament to how drunk I must have gotten last night if I told them about this place.

"I think any of them are fine. I never really did many grocery runs," I laugh, shuffling through last night's memories more time, trying to figure out how I agreed to return. It's not like I've had to go out of my way to avoid coming back. One does not simply stumble across the North Carolina coast unless they intend to. "Sorry, I'm still a bit out of it. After some coffee, I'll be the best local guide you can find." It's a lie coated in a thick layer of cheeriness. A trickle of anxiety reignites the roiling in my stomach.

I am not supposed to be here.

My ghosts here should have faded after four years. More specifically, they are in their first year of law school.

Still, it feels like there is a fist around my heart as the memories of my last visit start to flood to the surface.

Everything looks the same. The main street is lined with local businesses and restaurants with blue and yellow exteriors and delicate awnings. Each of them contains a part of my past.

Every quarter mile or so, signs declare, 'This way to the Beach!' despite pointing in contradictory directions. You couldn't pick a cuter beach town which is probably why my friends chose this place. I have no doubt they looked up 'Best Small Beach Town on the East Coast' and found it at the top of some list.

Libby leans over, "Are you doing ok? Like both physically and emotionally? I don't think I've ever seen anyone out drink Caleb and be functioning the next day." Functioning might be an overstatement for how I am fairing, physically or otherwise.

"I think the tequila cured me of any lingering feelings. Hibernating in the backseat definitely helped too." I give an attempt at a winning smile. I already crashed their plans. I don't want them worried about tip toeing around me the entire trip. "How are you not also wanting to crawl into a dark hole? You were with me all night."

"I had about twenty fewer drinks than you in my mission to keep you alive and get that asshole out of your system."

It's easy to be angry at Jackson, but it's also so easy for the hurt to seep in. I'm not the type of girl that gets casually cheated on. Isn't that what everyone says, though?

Literal supermodels have boyfriends that look like cartoon rats, and they still get cheated on.

What's worse is that it feels like I'm repeating history. Being cheated on is practically a Danes family tradition, and I guess it's finally my turn.

"This is the best time it could have happened. You're single on spring break. You're hot and going to the beach. There's plenty of opportunities for sloppy, meaningless hook-ups." Jess leans in from the middle seat.

I know she means well, but it's been less than twenty-four hours. I'd rather not think about any guy at the moment. Maybe I'll pick up a book and hide in a T-shirt all week.

But no, that's not fair. They invited me on the trip to have fun, so I'll try. If I try and it's miserable, then I'll hide.

I have to command myself to take deep breaths as the view outside of the car continues to stir the past.

This *will* be a relaxing, chill week. I can hang on by a thread if it means not ruining this.

My eyes are closed as I try to center myself when Caleb announces we've arrived.

"This place is perfect; the beach is literally the backyard," Josh says with the wide eyed expression of a child seeing an amusement park for the first time.

That was always the best part of summers here. You could roll out of the house and right into the water. I take one more moment to brace myself.

When I open my eyes, the torrent in my stomach becomes a hurricane. I needed to vomit.

We're at *my house*.

The house my parents sold before I went to college.

The thread holding me together starts to fray. I hate nostalgia, and I accidentally signed up for an entire week of it that I can't escape. I consider hunting down a car to the nearest airport so I can fly to my parent's house. Being home with my family during spring break might feel like purgatory compared to the fresh hell I am about to walk into.

The instant the front door is unlocked, I bolt into the downstairs bathroom. My body carries me there on instinct, not having to think about where I'm going. I've never been happier to be hungover and have an excuse for no one to chase after me. I could hide in the tiny downstairs toilet for the rest of the day, but I do have to face reality eventually.

I compose myself and find the guys preparing to brave the town for supplies. They have a handwritten list, courtesy of Jess and Amber's careful planning. I've seen their apartment.

If they go without instructions, we'd likely end up with cereal, beer, and burger patties— no buns.

Whenever I see my friends all in one place, I'm in awe of how we all fit together. Libby is a former track star that now prefers rock climbing and giving stick and poke tattoos or tarot readings at parties. Out of all of us, she hates the school part of college the most. She plans to work through Europe for the next few years. Trading time at farms and hostels for room and board.

Caleb grew up on a farm in Wyoming with four brothers. It's easy to see with his build that he grew up working. He is probably the dumbest smart person I know on track to graduate and build rockets for some tech company. When I asked why he chose aerospace engineering, he explained that he was good at blowing stuff up at the farm, so why not make a career out of it?

Jess looks like a Southern belle and has the matching accent, but with the mouth and mind to rival any teenage video gamer. Her big doe eyes and innocent look have gotten us out of more trouble than we had any right to be in. She'll be returning to New York to work on the design team for a new ecofriendly fashion brand. Our closets are full of sample styles and promotional gear.

Amber used to be Josh's tutor, assigned by the university to help him keep his football scholarship. She looked like someone who would be cast as the nerdy love interest in a romcom. The type where the movie fails to convince the audience that taking off her glasses and letting her hair down is a substantial makeover. He's now following to her medical school in California, where he plans on working as a consultant. We all secretly suspect that he has a ring tucked away in his underwear drawer.

We'd all met at various points during sophomore year. Everyone else seemed to have met their best friends for life freshman year, while we were left adrift. I love each of them so much that sometimes my heart hurts. I have missed us.

I'm struck by the reality of being here. This is our last spring break together, and I almost wasn't a part of it. We're about to head off to different sides of the world, and I almost gave this up for a guy whose movie theater snack was pretzels and who couldn't remember my drink order even after nearly two years.

We had all gone camping for spring break together sophomore year. Despite an incident with poison ivy, it is still one of the best trips of my life. After we got back, and over the spats that come from being stuck together in close quarters for a week, we promised to spend the rest of our spring breaks together.

I'm the only one who didn't follow through on the pact because weeks after we got back, I met Jackson. They weren't angry that I had chosen to go with Jackson and his friends last year, but it did start a rift between us. They never made me feel guilty about saying no to plans so I could spend more time with Jackson, but I felt the disconnect when I'd see pictures and hear inside jokes that I could have been a part of.

That entire time I had convinced myself that it was worth it. I had a healthy relationship that was important to prioritize. Now, the time I might have spent with them is just one more reason to be mad at myself about the breakup.

"We're getting coffee on the way back. Jess found a spot just a street away. Do you want anything?" Josh asks as they head to the door.

"A lavender honey latte would be great." It would probably be better to get something with mint or ginger for my stomach, but I can't resist.

"I'll text you if they don't have the ingredients for your signature drink," Josh promises.

"Or we could just stop by a soap store," Caleb jokes.

I nearly laugh because they are talking about the café where my obsession was born. I learned to make the drink at home with the espresso machine my parents got for my birthday years ago. Everyone thought it would taste like a candle. The general consensus was that the drink tasted like the best candle they'd ever had. None of them asked for another.

I finally take in the space.

The new owners have kept the same layout, and it even looks like they bought some of the furniture from my parents. Seeing the new and the old collide like this feels so wrong. Touristy posters and throws are mixed in with the cream, luxury couches my mom insisted on furnishing the place with.

Vases full of sea shells are on every major surface, just in case you forget the ocean is feet away. It feels fuller with bright colors and random knickknacks. Mom used to light candles with labels like 'linen' and 'clean.' Now, there is a little wall plug that might be pine scented. An odd choice for a beach house.

A painting of the shore done by a local artist used to take up the main wall of the living area. I always loved how the abstract brush strokes captured the movement of the water. I haven't seen it since the move. It could be in storage somewhere collecting dust, but it's more likely that they sold it.

My parents like to erase this place too.

The biggest change is the kitchen is no longer all crisp white. The cabinets have been replaced with light wood with a natural finish, likely a result of someone discovering the stain from a food coloring incident that first summer. We had taken bets on how long it would take my mother to notice. Apparently, it took a literal professional to get her into the kitchen long enough to even check. The space is far less sterile. It looks more lived in than it ever did when we were here.

Together, the changes make me feel less like I'm fourteen again and more like I've stepped into an alternate reality. *I've never been here before*, I tell myself. The thought isn't convincing.

The biggest benefit of the guys leaving is that Jess, Libby, Amber, and I get the first pick of the rooms. Amber grabs the old guest suite for her and Josh, which we're all grateful for as it's the furthest from the rest of the bedrooms.

Libby says she'll be fine on the couch. She often gets up at night and watches movies when she can't sleep. This way, she won't disturb anyone by going up and down the stairs. After living with her sophomore and junior year, I'm used to her nocturnal habits, but Amber is a light sleeper.

Jess picks the master for the two of us. This leaves Caleb with the designated kid's room, which has two twin beds and vinyl cartoon fish splattered across the walls. I am relieved that my old room has been converted into an office.

I had spent hours staring at that ceiling, sleepless but still dreaming of him. I can't bear the thought of anyone being in that space.

In the master, I sit on the bed, watching while Jess unpacks her suitcase. After attempting to unload my duffle, I decided that moving up and down to take things out of my bag would only induce more nausea.

"Honey, I'm home!" Josh's voice rings out, breaking through Libby's playlist, blaring over the speaker. Amber runs down the stairs and jumps on him, wrapping herself around him like a koala. It's a good thing he's a sturdy guy because her jump might have taken anyone else down.

They have that sickly sweet type of relationship that feels fake, and I only know how genuine it is because I've seen how much they used to hate each other. I lie to myself about the rancid feeling I get any time I see them together. My happiness for them battles resentment. I felt like this even when I was with Jackson.

"Here, Emma." Caleb is handing out our coffees, pulling my attention away. "They had actually had your order, even had it on the menu. It was called the Benjamin or something." I had left my phone downstairs, knowing he wouldn't have texted. Instead, I sip on liquid nostalgia and suppress thinking about the last time I was here doing this exact thing.

Once the groceries are packed away, everyone throws on swimsuits and races out to the beach. Well, everyone but me. I still need to pretend my aching body doesn't exist for a few hours.

It's still too cold to be in the water in early April, but that isn't enough to stop them. I hear a startled scream as someone crashes into the water. I sit on the couch for the rest of the day, rehydrating and streaming whatever pops up first on the TV. From my vantage point, I can see the water.

It's still and calm, hypnotic.

Late afternoon my phone rings. I'm expecting it to be Jackson, but it's my mother. I stopped checking for his texts

THE SUMMERS WE LEFT BEHIND

after the first few hours. But I still feel like one can pop up any minute.

The closer we get to graduation, the more frequent these unprompted motherly check-ins have started to become. We aren't a family that randomly calls 'just because.' Each conversation has a motive.

"Hey, Mom."

"Emma, I hope I'm not interrupting your plans with Jackson. I want to check in on what to tell your uncle. It's been a month since he gave you the job offer, and he needs to know if he should start interviewing other candidates." I haven't told her about the breakup, so she still thinks I'm in Tennessee. I plan to keep it that way as long as possible.

"Mom, that's not something I want to think about while I'm on vacation." It's something I've been avoiding thinking about at all. The Future. Something I used to feel like I had an endless amount of time to figure out, but it's snuck up on me.

"I'm sorry, but he needs an answer by the end of the week. You know you can pick which office to be located in? It could be good to talk to Jackson and plan things out. You could live together in New York. You have such a great future lined up." They love Jackson more than I ever did. He was stable, from a good family, and about to take a job in finance.

My parents hadn't been subtle the last time we visited them about their expectations and the future. They talked about ring sizes like I wasn't in the room.

I'll tell them after the break is over. Even if I explain that he cheated, I know they'll make it my fault. That *I* lost such a good partner. Despite its inevitability, I'm not ready for that right now.

"I'll call him in the next couple of days." It's better to just give in. It isn't worth fighting my mother and the now intensifying headache. I'm too busy with my past to think about the future.

With her victory, she hangs up.

My uncle has offered me a full time marketing position after interning for him the last two summers. Working for him is what my parents call 'family networking'— the rest of the world just calls it nepotism.

The job isn't anything that I'm passionate about, but at least I'm somewhat qualified. I was a mess going into school and picked the first major that looked like it would give me opportunities. Marketing seemed like the right choice.

I've carved the path, and now it doesn't seem like there's a way out. If I could go back, I'm not sure I would have chosen anything different.

My future has been handed to me at each stage of my life. I'm fine at school, but I never had to try for this. The offer feels flimsy, knowing it was a foregone conclusion this entire time and not something I've worked for. Maybe the opportunity would be more exciting if I had fought for the job. There was never any risk for the reward.

As the sun starts sinking, my friends return, dripping and tracking in a trail of sand. It'll be a bitch to clean up at the end of the trip, but I try not to fixate on it.

Remember, this is a fun-only zone.

A conch shell horn sounds in the distance, prompting my stomach to grumble with hunger.

Despite the fridge being full of food, we decide to get pizza delivered. After placing the order, Amber switches on a horror movie set on the beach. This choice is for Josh's benefit. Well, our benefit and Josh's begrudging acceptance.

He hates horror movies, but he loves Amber. More importantly, Amber loves watching him get scared shitless.

When the doorbell rings, Josh would have jumped out of his seat if it weren't for the blonde on his lap. Watching a 6'5" football player get freaked out over fake gore and zombie sharks is one of the little pleasures in life. Predictably, he uses answering the door as an excuse to avoid a few minutes of the movie.

We discovered his unrivaled ability to fall for jump scares on that first camping trip when Libby downloaded a movie about a serial killer that targeted young campers. It had freaked the rest of us out, but Josh wouldn't go anywhere alone for the rest of the trip. I wonder if they kept the themed horror movies for last spring break?

Though my friends may insist that there's never been anything wrong between us, I feel things starting to stitch back together as the credits roll. As the moment washes over me, I know I'm exactly where I'm supposed to be.

Being out in the sun combined with the long drive has drained everyone. They all stumble to their own corners of the house. But my body is wired after being dormant all day. Filled with pizza and about a gallon of water, I feel invigorated. If I go to bed now, I'll stay up staring at the ceiling with only my thoughts and Jess's snores as company.

I slide on my shoes and head out back. Up until this point, I've only seen the beach through the windows. My feet sink into the fine sand. Breathing in the salt air and hearing the rush of waves makes the world around me come into clear focus. Mentally, I'm still fighting the feeling of being back, but my body is happy to settle back into old habits. The tension in my shoulders and chest eases. It's like my body is reminding me that this is the place I'm supposed to be happy.

Holding my shoes in one hand, I step into the water. The chill of it grounds me, numbing my feet until I'm not sure where the ocean starts and I end. I look over to see strings of lights twinkling from the neighbor's house. The lights are still on inside, emanating a soft glow. A group of people are mingling in what I know is the living room.

Even if one of the partygoers looks my way, they won't be able to see me well enough to pick out my features.

Someone in the upstairs window looks out at the ocean for a moment before shifting out of view. I try and convince my heart not to crash through my ribs as I think about whose room that is.

He isn't here. That's not even a possibility.

Standing here, staring at the empty window, I can only think of the first boy I ever loved.

2

Summer

Eight years ago

I can tell we're getting close by the taste of the air. I lower the car window, letting the wind whip through my curls, even though I know I'll regret this later when I have to manage the tangles. But for now, I get lost in the freedom of it.

The town zips by as we pass colorful shops and tourist signs. I take note of which ones I want to visit later.

Our house is right on the water. My mother showed me pictures of it on the drive up, but the realtor's site didn't do the house or the town justice.

The house is gorgeous, but it's like they asked someone to design a beach house without ever going to the beach. Compared to the other houses, ours is out of place. Too crisp and white. It's also too big, but my mother insists we'll want the space when my father and Corrina visit.

The summer house was supposed to be my big surprise before starting high school. I'm pretty sure that my mother was just getting sick of summertime in D.C. when interns and tourists flood in. Every year she grumbles about the traffic and the college students blocking the sidewalks with all their gawking.

We go our separate ways once we get inside. She starts to unload the grocery delivery as I rush up the stairs.

I find the door to my new room immediately. The inside is taken from a magazine. I mean a literal magazine. My mother probably picked an entire predesigned room and had it set up. The bedspread is embroidered with shells, and the décor could generally be classified as cozy nautical. It feels more like a themed hotel suite than the room I'm supposed to consider mine.

The moment I set down my last bag, my eyes are on the beach.

"Remember not to track sand into the house. I only have the cleaners coming once a week," my mother calls out.

The beach is our backyard. We've never had a backyard before. My dad always insisted having a yard was not worth the work. I shed clothes as I rush for the back door.

In anticipation, I had worn my swimsuit for the six hour drive. I kick off my sandals into the sand and run into the ocean.

We've gone to the beach once before when Corrina begged to go to the amusement parks in Florida. I was too young to remember anything about the trip. My parents claim that beaches were too packed and loud, full of screaming kids, and littered with trash. Despite what they say, Corrina swears it was one of our best trips as a family.

One time she dug up an old photograph as proof. When I looked at it, I didn't recognize the smiling family.

I was always jealous whenever the girls from school returned with summer tans. They always looked so carefree and natural. As if the energy of vacation followed them into the school year. I can't wait to walk in this year feeling the same way.

The beach is an entirely different world. It's an hour before the sunset, and the horizon's full of golden, dancing light. The world is glowing.

I stand at the water's edge, soothing my feet from the brief run across the scorching sand. When I think about taking another step, my mind drifts to thoughts about hidden poisonous fish and sharp teeth. I stay put, watching the water swirl just above my ankles.

No one else is on this stretch of shore, but I can see umbrellas in the distance. I'm left to enjoy the sun reflecting off the water alone. I'm so entranced that I don't hear any footsteps.

"Are you just going to stand there or actually get in?" I jump at the voice. I turn to face a boy about my own age. His sandy brown hair falls lazily across his forehead, and a spattering of freckles kisses his cheeks. As he moves closer, I can see that his eyes are the color of honey left out in the sun, catching the light from the last rays of the day.

"I don't know." I don't want to admit that I'm intimidated by the ocean. I've heard stories of people being carried away by riptides and terrible jellyfish stings. The idea of a beach house had been so exciting that I forgot about my worries until I was actually in the water. I promise myself that I will get in eventually. "Do you live around here?" I ask, trying to shift the conversation.

"Yup," he says, popping the last letter. "I live in the pink house right there." He points and then lowers himself to the ground next to me. The house he pointed to is to the right of ours. Side by side, they look like two sisters determined to have polar opposite styles. The Pink House has a tangle of lights unevenly wrapped along the deck railing; mismatched chairs circle a table with a lone forgotten soda can resting on top.

"We just moved in next door." I am suddenly conscious of my mess of curls, wild and tangled from sticking my head out the window on the drive in. I try to tuck some of my unruly strands behind my ears, but on the third attempt, I give up.

"Oh, thank god. There was this family with like three babies that almost bought it," he says. I laugh at his reply, glad that I am the one that found him and not some rouge child. My eyes travel to the faint scar on his lip as he talks. It's stark against his summer tanned skin.

"I'm Bennett, by the way." He sticks out his hand but doesn't rise.

"You don't go by Ben?" I take his hand, then sit down next to him.

"No. I never saw the point in having a full name just to shorten it. My parents don't either." His eyes widen, "Don't tell me you're one of those people who have to give everyone nicknames. If you are, we might have to cut this friendship very short."

I giggle.

Friendship. I like how he tosses the word around. I've never talked to a boy like this. "No nicknames here. I'm Emma. I don't really have enough name to shorten it to anything." I don't tell him that Emma is short for Emma Claire. My double name feels too heavy at the beach. Here, I'm just going to be Emma.

"You could totally just go by Em. You could make it work, but I like Emma." I've never been given a nickname, but right then, Bennett makes me feel like I don't need one. A conch shell horn rings from the porch of the Pink House. "Mom's calling for dinner. I'll see you soon, okay?" The question feels more like a promise, making me giddy for the rest of the summer.

The next day, someone knocks at our door. It's nine in the morning, which is basically seven in summer time. I am still eating a bowl of cereal when I answer. My mother is upstairs, in a deep sleep from whatever she took last night.

She can't sleep through the night without whatever the doctor prescribes.

"Hey." I can't help but beam at the sight of Bennett in my doorway. The boy who lives in the Pink House.

"Umm, here. My mom insisted I bring them over just in case you didn't have anything for breakfast. They're orange cardamom." He holds out a heaping basket of muffins. The sweet and spicy smell of the muffins is irresistible. Even though I'm already eating, my stomach grumbles.

It will take a week to get through them, if not longer. Mom is on a smoothie kick, and there is a large chance she won't touch them. I feel guilty accepting something like this, knowing it won't be fully appreciated. This gift should be savored.

"Thank you. These look amazing. She made these?" I note the pride on his face when I ask.

"Yeah, she was surprised to hear you guys moved in. My mom usually knows who's coming into town before anyone else. She wanted me to tell you she's planning a better housewarming gift. I think she'll be over later once she opens up the shop."

"I'm not sure when my mom will be up, and my dad won't be here until the weekend. What kind of shop is it?"

"They have the bakery and coffee shop just a street over. I'm not sure if you saw it coming in, Early Bird Café?"

"Oh, it has that swing out front." I fell in love with that swing the moment I set eyes on it. I imagine spending hours sipping on iced coffee and reading a good book, despite the fact I haven't picked up a non-school related book for years and don't really care much for coffee. But I'm here to find a new version of myself. I am excited for lazy days, where time moves differently.

"That's the one. You should stop by. I'm helping out this afternoon if you want to say hi." He runs his hand through his hair, looking nervous that I'll tell him no. But there's nothing I want to do more.

"Really? I'd love to!"

After Bennett leaves, I sift through the piles of clothes I've yet to unpack. Nothing feels right. It all still feels like the city. Where did I think I'd be wearing this many skirts?

I settle on a pair of shorts and a faded shirt I usually just sleep in. It's all so comfortable. That's what I want this place to be, comfortable. Hopefully, the house will look lived in after a couple of weeks, but I have no intention of staying stuck inside all summer.

I had begged for a bike. Whenever I think of being in a beach town, I picture bikes and pedestrians instead of heavy traffic. Mine is what the bike shop website calls a cruiser. It's banana yellow in a swoopy retro style with a little basket on the front. I find it in the garage, along with a floral helmet.

The problem with my plan is that I don't actually know how to ride a bike. How hard can it be?

The answer is really hard. I fall three times on my way to the coffee shop. Each time making it no more than a few feet. There is a scrape on my knee and definitely a bruise forming on my hip. The basket looks a little scraped up, but I took most of the damage. I end up walking most of the way to Early Bird.

A little bell jingles as I push through the café door. The far wall has enough exposed brick to be the envy of any artist's loft. An assortment of plush, vintage-looking furniture presents the picture of casual comfort. The atmosphere is so inviting.

I walk up to the counter, my eyes lingering on every detail until my gaze falls on Bennett, who is in the same clothes as this morning. The only difference is now he's wearing a baseball cap with the Early Bird logo, a cartoon bird holding a mug of coffee.

"Emma!" He returns my smile, but his face falls when he sees my banged up legs. "What happened? Did you fight a stray dog or something?" I don't want to answer that just yet. I want to be friends with him, and the whole bike scenario might end any chance of that.

"Who is this?" A cheery woman wearing a flour covered apron comes up next to Bennett. She's blonde with touches of grey tucked under a cap identical to Bennett's. It's easy to see that she's his mom. They have the same smile and honey eyes.

"Mom, this is Emma. Emma, this is my mom."

"It's great to meet you, Mrs...." Bennett never told me his last name. So, now I'm left hanging. My mind goes blank trying to figure out how to recover. I throw him a panicked look. *Help Me.*

"Sorenson," Bennett jumps in.

"Oh, just call me Diane. We have first names for a reason. Why shouldn't we use them?" She echoes a version of what Bennett said last night. She looks over to her son, "You didn't say how pretty she was." He flushes. I stiffen as heat crawls all over my neck and face. "Coffee on the house today." She wanders away, throwing a wink over her shoulder.

"So, what can I get you?" He breaks the awkward pause between us.

"Just an iced coffee."

"Anything in it?" I shake my head. "You're kidding me, right?"

My parents only ever order it black, so I've never tried it any other way.

One look at the menu and the flavors are all foreign to me. Rose and cinnamon? How can that taste like anything other than soap? The sea salt option feels appropriately beachy, but I'm not sure it belongs in a drink.

"I'm making you my favorite then. I'm going to change how you drink coffee forever." He moves to the chrome espresso machine and starts a latte, forgoing the iced coffee altogether.

He works the machine with practiced ease, not looking as he flies through the process. He throws in at least three different syrups and an oat milk that is labeled 'extra creamy.'

"I give you the honey lavender latte with a touch of cinnamon, or The Bennett." He presents it with a flourish.

"That sounds like a candle." I'm scared I'll spit it out if I don't like it.

I already don't love coffee. I really only like the idea of coffee.

"No, you're not allowed to say anything until you try it." He holds up a hand, sensing my wariness.

Under his unrelenting attention, I take a sip. "I hate that you're right. It's perfect." It's light and fresh; the floral taste is subtle and is complimented by the sweetness of the honey. I pull out my wallet to pay.

"Absolutely not. My mom will kill me if I let you pay for this," he says. So, I shove the five dollar bill in the tip jar and run outside before he can protest.

I have achieved two parts of the coffee shop dream. All I need is a book. I don't even know what I like to read. A book just feels necessary.

I still have my bike, so finding a bookstore will have to be an adventure for later. Walking my bike everywhere around town will ruin my already trampled pride. And I'm happy with the two parts of perfect I've already snatched up.

I have no idea how much time passes before Bennett's shift is over. But when he comes outside and finds me, he seems shocked, "You're still here." He looks over at the bike. "Oh, that's how you got all banged up. Did you run into something?"

I'm blushing again. "I fell off a few times. I don't actually know how to ride one. I just never learned. I know it's stupid, but I thought it would be easy. If kids can figure it out, why can't I?" Once the words start flowing, I can't stop them. Something about him makes me want to tell him everything.

"No, that makes sense. I can teach you if you want to try again," he offers, nodding as if everything I just said is perfectly understandable.

"Thanks, but maybe not today, though."

"What else do you have going on? What's stupid is giving up after one try."

Thirty minutes later, we are back on our street, his hands on my waist keeping me from falling. I kept getting distracted by his touch supporting me. Isn't he supposed to hold onto the handlebars, or something else?

"Woah, eyes on the road," he says. I hadn't noticed the pothole I'd just run over because I was looking over my shoulder at him. After another few laps, he asks, "You ready for a solo ride?"

"Yeah, I think I have the hang of it," I answer. He lets go, which is nearly as startling as when he first touched me. I peddle furiously, coasting once I've gotten enough speed. The wind starts flowing by, catching my hair. "I'm doing it!" I yell. I look back and then promptly crash into a mailbox.

Bennett walks my bike back as I wince with each step I take. I am made of bruises and road rash.

I might be more excited about finally going into the Pink House if my body didn't feel shredded from the asphalt.

We spend the rest of the afternoon icing my knee and watching reruns on the TV.

When I get up to get more ice, I notice the contents of the house. It's full of the little things that let you know it's a home, not just a stopping place. Pictures are scattered on every surface, capturing notable events and touristy vacations.

An older photo looks like it's of a younger Diane and a man that must be Bennett's father. Her arms are flung over his neck, and they look like they are about to topple over with joy.

I've only seen one picture from my parent's wedding. It was beautiful, with cascading flowers and a perfectly flowing dress train. But it looked staged, like a museum display or magazine ad titled 'The Happy Couple.'

On the way into the kitchen, I see a doorway showing the heights of Bennett and two others marked with their initials,

'B.S.,' T.S.,' and 'J.S..' After my self-guided tour, I settle back into the couch.

"Wow, when did Benny get a girlfriend?" A group of guys a year or two older than us clamber in from the beach side of the house.

"She's just our neighbor. They moved in yesterday." I am thankful Bennett says something as I sink further into the couch. I've felt very seen today by people I don't know. Turning invisible feels like an amazing idea.

"Well, if she's not your girlfriend." The guy offers a wink, and I'm unsure if I can turn a deeper shade of red. I know he's joking, but that makes it worse.

"Shove off, Tanner." I'm still recovering as they head to a different part of the house.

"I'm sorry about my brother. He can be a dick."

"It's fine."

The second time I meet Tanner, I'm surprised took me so long to see the resemblance. They have the same messy hair and square jaw. Where Bennett's looks made him appear easygoing and inviting, Tanner looks rougher, the lines of his face sharp. He has darker brown eyes and a slightly crooked nose that looks like it has been broken and wasn't set properly.

"Stare much?" He says between bites of his pizza. Bennett had invited me over for dinner and movies, so we're all gathered in the living room.

"I'm making scientific observations." My eyes continue to shift between the brothers, cataloging the differences.

"Bennett, I take back what I said. You can keep her."

"I was never up for grabs." I throw a stray piece of pepperoni at him. It flies through the air and sticks to his forehead with a *thwack* before he peels it off and pops it into his mouth.

"Thanks for the snack."

Throughout the evening, Tanner and I continue to trade verbal jabs, settling into knowing each other.

It rains the rest of that first week. It's a light sprinkle in the mornings that turns into an afternoon torrent.

On one of these mornings, I discover a new and used bookshop a quick bike ride away. During the ride, I'm so proud of myself for finally accomplishing what most people do as preschoolers.

The shop has no name, just a big sign that says 'Books.' It's more of a declaration of what waits inside than a name.

I walk in to find one shop attendant, three if you include the two cats that demand attention by tripping you. The sections are written on index cards with looping handwriting that I can't quite interpret. There's a staff recommendations section that looks like the employees put on a blindfold and chose the first thing they touched. I'm serious. There's a cookbook. Who recommends a cookbook?

Each time I return, I decide to pick a book from a new section. It gives me a good guess of what each section is actually supposed to be. After the third book, I start relabeling the shelves replacing the illegible index cards with my own that likely have limited accuracy but are at least easy to read.

When I ask Bennett about the store, he tells me that it's been there since before he was born, and the old man who runs it had a name for it at some point. But a nasty storm trashed the sign. So now, all the people in town just call it Books since there isn't another bookstore, which is likely why Books is still in business.

A week later, my cards are still up, so either I have similar handwriting to an employee, or the cats are the only ones perusing the shelves with any regularity.

I always make my way to Early Bird after Books. I usually have what Bennett made for me that first time. On other days, he will give me his newest creations.

"May I present to you: Swamp Water."

"Why is it green?" I scrunch my nose.

"Mom got matcha, and I've been playing around with it. Turns out that when you mix it with espresso, it turns the color of swamp water. I swear it's better than it looks." He is always right. Maybe he's an excellent barista, or maybe I just like it because he's the one making it.

Coffee in hand, I curl up on the swing. I usually make it through half a book by the time Bennett gets off. I get through mystery, horror, nonfiction, a Jane Austen novel, and romance that first week. I'm not expecting what will unfold when I open that romance book.

The cover is so unassuming, just a picture of a dock and the bright blue ocean behind it. The title, *Whispering Cove*, is printed in slanting cursive.

I know about sex, obviously; I'm about to go into high school. My mom sat me down and had a vague talk a year ago. My friends are so excited about the prospect of boys and dating that they talk about it whenever they get the chance, but I just didn't get it. This book makes it sound like the most earth-shattering experience any woman can have. Still, I can't put it down.

I'm flushed by the time Bennett walks out to find me. I slam the book shut like I've been caught doing something scandalous. It only makes me look more suspicious.

"What do you have there?" Before I can stop him, he snatches the book and opens it to where I stopped. He stares at the pages, and instantly, his eyes widen. Red stains his cheeks. He sits down, pulling a pillow onto his lap. "I think my mom told me she was reading this. Knowing that the three of us have this shared experience, I'm thoroughly scarred." I really didn't need to know that.

"You ready to go?" I can't leave this moment fast enough.

"Umm, actually, I think I need a minute. Work really knocked it out of me."

When neither of us says anything, I flip the back book open. I don't know what drives me to do it, but it feels powerful when I see the shock roll through Bennett's features.

I don't pick up another romance book after I finish *Whispering Cove*, but it remains forever burned into my memory. We never talk about the contents of the pages we've seen, but knowing Bennett saw them and was just scandalized makes me feel less awkward.

3

Summer

Eight years ago

Whenever I run out of things to do or need company, Bennett is always there. It's like he has a sense for when I want to go on our next adventure, even if that adventure is just a walk by the water, collecting freckles.

"There's a bonfire on the beach tonight. You should come," Bennett says.

"Like with your family?" I love spending time at his house. A bonfire with them sounds perfect.

"It's some of the local people I know from school." I adore his family, but I'm less sure about other people. I have school friends, but they're just that, friends at school. Those friendships never extend any further.

"Ok."

"I promise you'll fit right in. If you can get Tanner to like you, they shouldn't be a challenge," he reassures me.

"Are you sure?"

He holds out his hand with his pinkie extended to me. "Promise."

"You're serious right now."

"Dead serious."

"I was five last the time I made a pinkie promise."

"Pinkie promises are no child's play. Do you know what they actually mean?"

"No. Enlighten me." I roll my eyes, our fingers still linked.

"It means that if either of us breaks the promise, the other is allowed to break that person's finger. It is a promise that is more than words." For emphasis, he finally releases my pinkie.

"Do people wear shoes to these things?" I blurt. It's the stupidest thing I can ask, but I need to know. This is different from other summer things I'd gone to back home or just being here around town.

He laughs, but not in a way that makes me embarrassed about my question. "Sandals and probably a sweatshirt. It can get cold when the sun goes down. I've got to go back to the shop to help my mom with something, but I'll stop by before I walk over."

It's just after eight when he picks me up. I do a slow spin once we're out the door.

"Do I meet the dress code requirements?" I'd feel silly showing off my tie dye sweatshirt and shorts for anyone else, but he isn't just anyone.

He makes a show, careful of inspecting the outfit, stepping around me, and making hmming sounds. "I think it's passable. Not MET gala worthy, but definitely on theme."

Approaching the beach, I see a few smaller fires where groups are gathered. Somewhere, a speaker plays music. People wander between the fires. A few couples have already run off to more secluded corners where the firelight barely touches.

We have run into people Bennett and the Sorensons know every time we are out, but it still shocks me how many people call out to him now. It has only been us for the last couple of weeks, and I've never considered that I could be monopolizing his time. I feel honored and guilty in a weird twist of emotion. He can spend time with any of these people but still chooses me.

"Hey, Sorenson," A guy sitting next to one of the fires calls out to us. Well, to Bennett, not me.

"Emma, these are the guys. Davis, Andre, and Justin. Emma moved in next door for the summer," Bennett introduces everyone.

Davis is a lanky, dark haired boy on the far end of the log. The one that called us over is Andre, whose smile is blindly white against his dark features. Justin has spiky hair that makes him look like he's just touched a live wire; he is currently hyper-focused on roasting a marshmallow.

"Hi." I give a weak smile. They all seem nice enough.

"Shit." Justin's marshmallow is now engulfed in flame.

"Ok, you're officially off s'mores duty," Andre cackles, yanking the roasting stick from Justin. Upon closer inspection, a handful of charred clumps are in the fire.

Bennett takes over. He assembles the fireside snacks with the same casual yet intentional care he does with drinks in the café.

I settle next to Davis on the log turned bench. He seems like the tamest of the group, like if you let him, he'll fade into the shadows. That's how I feel a lot of the time too.

"So, where you from?" Davis asks before the silence between us stretches too long.

"D.C., my mother wanted a change of pace this year. You're local?"

"Yeah, we all go to school together. Does that mean you go to museums all the time?"

"Why does everyone ask that?"

"Hey, they're just jealous museums because are cool."

"I don't think I've ever heard someone over ten and under sixty say that out loud." I laugh, but I see his expression and add, "I like them, though. I spent last summer trying to pick my favorite display from each exhibit in the National Gallery. I have a color-coded spreadsheet and everything. I'll show you my list sometime." I knock his knee with mine.

A shiver runs through me. Bennett was right; it does get cold, and even with my sweatshirt and the fire, I'm a bit chilly. I've always run a bit cold, but for some reason, I assumed the beach would just cancel that out.

"Here," Davis offers a bit of the blanket on his lap.

Bennett plops down next to me with three perfectly constructed s'mores. His eyes flicker to the shared blanket as he hands out his creations.

Throughout the night, the dynamic settles into place. Bennett and Andre are bright and joking with everything they do. Occasionally, Justin makes an abrupt and unrelated change to the conversation. Still, they always make a point to include me and Davis. People aren't forgotten here.

"Ready to head back? I've got an early shift tomorrow and should probably get some sleep," Bennett leans in. I haven't felt much time pass, but looking at my phone, I see we've been out for hours. Once I know the time, my eyelids grow heavy, the exhilaration of the night draining from me.

"Sure." I shift out from under the blanket, thanking Davis. We say our goodbyes and head home.

"I can tell they really liked you," Bennett tells me.

"Really?"

"Without a doubt." He flashes a toothy grin, and the tension releases from my chest.

We see the guys and a few other of their friends throughout the summer, but our dynamic stays the same. It is mostly just the two of us, and once a week or so, we meet up with a group to go to the movie theater a town over or play volleyball.

On one notable occasion, Andre spikes a ball right into my face and then declares that he will protect me from that ever happening again. From that point on, we are always on the same team. I have a place here.

I know Bennett has something planned whenever he knocks on the front door. If he just wants to spend time together, he'll tap on the glass in the back door or find me on Early Bird's porch. This time when I open the door, he jumps right into his proposal for the day.

"Here's the deal. It's my mom's birthday this weekend. I lost the coin flip, so I'm making the cake. Could I please make it at your place? I want to surprise her this year," he begs.

"Only if I get to be your sous chef."

"I'm not sure they have sous chefs for bakers, but I think we can make an exception this one time."

"Ok, it's a deal." I extend my pinkie, and we shake on it.

"The concept: The Ocean." He is so proud of himself, but I can't suppress the snort that escapes.

"You're serious?" I don't point out that my seven-year-old cousin's birthday was the last time I saw an ocean themed cake.

"It's not original, but my brothers always do something with coffee or just pink. So, for the Sorenson boys, this is revolutionary."

"Well, then, let's make history."

It turns out that an ocean themed cake involves a lot of blue food coloring. Each layer of the cake has more coloring added in an attempt to make it look like the water is getting deeper. We make waves out of icing and scatter edible pearls. A big 'Happy Birthday Diane' is scrawled across the top, my handiwork.

"She's going to love it. I can't wait for you to tell me what she thinks," I say, taking in the final product.

"What do you mean? She can tell you herself since you're coming to the party." He looks genuinely confused that I thought I wouldn't be invited. It's the warmest feeling to be unconditionally welcomed.

We had been so focused on our masterpiece that we didn't notice the mess. When we look around the room, the stark white of the kitchen is now splattered with blue dye and vanilla cake batter.

"Shit," we say in unison.

We scrub using the sparse array of cleaning products we keep in the house. After getting most of it out, there is still a stubborn streak on the cabinet above the sink. I convince myself that the blue blends into the white enough that you can't see it if you don't look hard.

Bennett cleans himself up, then comes over to pick up the cake and me the next evening, just as the sky begins to streak with cotton candy colors over the water. He's found a dish cover to orchestrate a grand reveal.

He's careful not to trip as we make our way up the stairs to the deck. He sets down the tray and reveals the cake with a flourish. One side of the icing is slightly messed up from it bumping into the cover.

Diane loves it, dented icing and all. She hugs us both before taking an entire album's worth of pictures on her phone.

The party is on the back deck of the Sorenson house, with guests strewn about. The deck is so full that the crowd trickles onto the shore. The entire town is coming in and out. The only decorations are strings of lights and a handmade birthday banner Tanner painted, which he makes certain everyone knows.

This is the first time I've seen all of the Sorensons together. The oldest Sorenson brother, Jones, has flown in from Missouri. Richard is always there for dinner when I join, but this is the first time I've seen him outside of a meal. He cooks while Diane bakes; it's a hard and fast rule. One time he tried to make pizza, and Diane pushed him out of the kitchen, telling him it was her job. Both men are less boisterous than the rest of their family. I don't think Harriettesville could handle five loud, energetic Sorensons.

Their family is a unit that makes so much sense. A glow radiates when they are all together, wrapping everyone else around them in a warm hug. They joke and fight, but it's always punctuated with laughter and genuine smiles.

Looking at them makes me ache and long for this to be mine. My own mother's birthdays are spent at spas or retreats that scream, 'I'm happier by myself.' I'm determined not to let thoughts of comparison take hold and dampen my mood. Bennett has taken my hand and brought me into this sanctuary.

I will not take this for granted. *This is what happiness looks like.* I tuck the thought away for when I need it again.

The party continues to overflow with joy and laughter long into the night.

After a game of cards with more empty threats than strategy, Bennett and I walk down to the shore. Water rolls over our feet as we make footprints in the wet sand. I'm that satisfied type of tired that takes hold when your body can't take any more laughter.

"I want to have a party like this one day," I say as I lean into Bennett.

"I promise you will."

I believe him.

I had been so excited for the Fourth of July. My anticipation is ruined when a summer cold has me glued to the couch the morning of the Fourth. Diane drops off tea and soup that morning. My mother left yesterday, headed home for some charity event. I sleep most of the day, hoping the stuffy nose and cough will pass.

The sun is still up as the first cracks of fireworks fill the air. The colors of the explosives battle the rays of the sun. As the sun starts to dip below the horizon, the brilliant, sparkling fireworks are mesmerizing, accented by the scattered hues of sunset.

After I settle back onto the couch with a new bowl of soup, there is a loud tapping at the back door. Bennett is looking, holding up a plate loaded up with a burger and chips.

"What are you doing here?" I ask as I let him in.

"You shouldn't be alone on a holiday," he says like it's Christmas or Thanksgiving.

"Fourth of July isn't a big deal."

"It absolutely is. It's a friend holiday. You're supposed to be around people. I would be a bad friend if I left you in here alone."

"I'll get you sick," I protest.

"No, you won't. I never get sick. Let's go watch the fireworks."

I follow him onto the deck. We sit on the edge, letting our legs dangle through the gaps in the railing. The soup was amazing, but the burger is practically perfect.

"You know what this is missing?" I ask, taking a massive bite.

"Tell me."

"Pineapple."

"Excuse me?"

"You have your weird drinks; I have my perfect burger topping."

"I'll make sure we have it next time, then."

The fireworks in D.C. are undeniably a spectacle, but after fourteen years, the choreographed display has lost its luster.

Seeing the explosions on the beach for the first time leaves me speechless. Nothing can compare to how they reflected in a thousand fragments across the water. The recklessness of the entire community shooting off their rockets adds a thrill that can't be captured by the carefully curated display I'm accustomed to.

For the rest of the night, my focus flickers between Bennett and the fireworks. I can't decide which view I like more.

Three days later, Bennett is sick on the couch, and I'm the one bringing him food.

It's mid-July before I seriously get in the water. After a month and a half, the deepest I've gone is up to my knees, and even then, I jumped out when a stray plant wrapped around my ankle.

"We have to get you over this fear of getting into the water. You've been here for too long not to enjoy the whole experience," Bennett says.

"Fine, you go first. I'll follow you in."

He wades in only waist deep. "See, it's fine." Then in a jerk of movement, it looks like he trips and goes under. My heart races. I almost scream for help just as he breaks through the surface again with a huge grin.

"That's not funny. I was about to call for help." I start to step closer to him. My eyes don't leave my feet, hyper aware of what could lurk beneath the sand.

"I'm wounded. You wouldn't have come in to save me?" If there had been actual trouble, I wouldn't have been able to do much about it. My eyes are still on the water, not paying attention to how close I've gotten until I bump into him. I stumble and jolt as he catches me.

"Hey, it's just me," he soothes, not knowing that his touch is the reason for my jumpiness. "And look." Another thing I've missed from being so preoccupied with the sand beneath my feet is that he's lured me out further. He had slowly taken steps back, like how you teach a toddler to swim. You can trick them because they trust you.

Bennet is knocking on the back door, drawing my attention away from my latest mystery novel. He's clutching a bundle of empty trash bags and two alligator grips used to pick things up.

"Let's go. I'm going to show you what I do when I'm not working morning shifts."

"I'm not exactly dressed for adventure right now." I look down at my blue cotton pajamas and house slippers. But he doesn't relent. "Give me five minutes, and I'll be good to go. I can meet you wherever."

"Nah, I'm staying right here and timing you." I scramble up as he pulls out his phone to start the timer. I know he'll wait even if I take more than five minutes, but playing along is more fun.

After splashing my face with water, throwing on a swimsuit, then wiggling into jean shorts and a tank top, I am practically wheezing. I almost don't make the last step as I sprint back down the stairs, having to clutch the railing not to tip over.

"Four minutes flat, nice hustle Danes."

Apparently, Bennett spends his free mornings cleaning up the beach.

"You just brought me along for free labor," I whine. Harriettesville has much cleaner beaches than other places I've seen, but the tourists still leave it strewn with wrappers and cans. Despite my words, I don't mind helping. This is a place I enjoy caring for.

"Are you questioning my motivations?" He is attentive as we make our way down the beach, always looking for the shine of aluminum or a buried scrap.

After walking and filling our bags for about an hour, he reaches for something that I expect to be more trash, but he holds out his hands to show a cloudy blue piece of glass formed into an oblong triangle. I've seen pictures of sea glass before but never found any, despite hours of looking.

"I know picking up trash kind of sucks. But finding stuff like this makes it worth it."

"Does it ever feel pointless when you come back and see that there's more?"

"No, it's just more reason to try. I can't stand not working to keep places like this clean and healthy. I was thinking about becoming a marine scientist, but after I took a biology class last year and I just didn't get it, I've started looking at other options. Environmental law looks cool. Mom says I've always been good at fighting for people. I don't really get what she means, but if I can make this work, I can fight for the world in my own way."

I reach for his hand and say, "If I know anything about you, Bennett Sorenson, it's that you go for what you want, and there is nothing out there to stop you."

His wistful look shifts into something I can't read as he shifts his gaze from the ocean to me. "There are plenty of things out there that I'm not sure how to get. Sometimes trying is the most terrifying thing in the world." We stand there looking out, not moving, trash bags in hand.

When I comment on our full bags, Bennett launches into the impact of tourism on the environment, "Mom loves tourist season, though. Without it, we couldn't keep the café running like it does all year round. She also says living where people vacation, you get to stay in one place while all the interesting people come to you. My least favorite is spring break. The college students leave so many cans everywhere. But sometimes we get lucky, and they forget cases of beer, so that makes up for it.

I don't realize how fast our first summer here has flown by until we're loading our bags into the car in August. As my mother checks the house for anything she might have left behind, Bennett rushes around the corner.

"I almost forgot. I need your phone number. I'm sorry. I mean, can I get it?" We have seen each other every day, and it slipped my mind that we never texted or called. We just showed up. If he hadn't come over, I could have potentially not talked to him for a year. Now that I know Bennett Sorenson, there is no way I could have gone that long without having him in my life.

So many things are the same. My father never showed up. The house is still empty. My mother and I never grew a deep and meaningful bond over our time together.

But still, something important has shifted. Being in Harriettesville for the summer has sparked something in me to meet people who make me feel alive.

Cammie is just that. She is so full of life. From the first time I meet her in Freshman English, she is just a bit too loud for whatever room she is in, but she never dims herself whenever someone points it out. I love her loudness; it drowns out the monotony of everything else.

Her parents are artists who spent summers abroad or at creative retreats. She pours out stories, crafting elaborate explanations about the most mundane things.

She becomes my shelter from the dull constant of life at home and the drudge of school. She invites me to galleries for new artists her parents meet. They are fresh and bright compared to the events my parents drag me to.

"I want to be you when I grow up," I tell her one day.

"I'm not sure how that's supposed to work since you're a month older than me." She laughs.

It's true, though. I'm just starting to know myself. Having that one summer away from the city woke me up. Cammie has the energy of someone that's known herself from a young age. I want to be like that.

4
Sunday
Now

Few things are better than waking up without a hangover after suffering from the mind-clouding, stomach-turning feeling the day before. I'm born again, and despite the initial shock of the summer house, I know the rest of the trip will be full of brilliant sunsets and relaxation.

It's easy to spend a week being a beachgoer, and I'll be content with doing just that. Sitting on the beach means I can stare out into the distance and let my mind clear of any thoughts of boys and frayed friendships.

In early April, being on a beach in Harriettesville requires layers of clothing and, sometimes, blankets that are doomed to never be free of sand. Still, plenty of people are leaping in and out of the water. Back home, sixty degrees is still perfect for a sweater. Here, I am in shorts and an unzipped hoodie over my swimsuit.

The beach lets us lie to ourselves, saying Everything is perfect. Why wouldn't it be? We are too eager to believe it, and in turn, we purposefully overlook the rough edges of reality that would be too sharp anywhere else.

Jess and I are the only ones not trying to force our bodies to acclimate to the cold water. Her box braids are secured in a bun, and she has one earbud in. She never commits to both headphones just in case someone wants to talk.

"You need a rebound. This place isn't overflowing with hot beach people like Miami or LA, but there are plenty to pick from. Look at him. He seems fine." Jess points to a dark haired man with mirrored sunglasses. He's definitely attractive, but she's overlooking something very important.

"Jess, that guy is literally with a girl right now, and it doesn't look like they're siblings," I say.

The man in question is rubbing sunscreen on a girl's back, paying very close attention to detail. It's a bad habit of Jess's to look at a guy and not notice the important things like the girlfriend on his phone lock screen or a wedding ring. It's never intentional. She just sees attractive guys as a four course meal and forgets to check if they're even on the menu.

She craves love, and it comes easy to her. The only reason she has not been with anyone long term is that no one meets her standards. When Jess doesn't think she's getting what she deserves, she moves on. I know the person she'll end up with will be perfect. It's not a possibility she won't find the perfect person; she was born to be loved.

"Ok, then what about him." She points in the other direction, where a group of guys are passing a volleyball. "He is so perfectly your type; it's criminal."

She is spot on.

He is my type. Tall, lean, skin tanned from being out in the sun, sandy brown hair that has a soft wave. What I can't see from this distance are the honey colored eyes and the small scar on his lip that stands out after he's spent an entire day outside.

He's the standard that I've held all past relationships and hookups against. Jess really has a talent for picking guys.

I thought I'd gotten past the anxiety-inducing energy of being back here, but with just one look at him, my heart is threatening to beat out of my chest and onto the sand.

I feel the blood drain from my face, freezing despite the soft warmth of the sun. "I think I have my first two day hangover. I still feel so gross. I'm headed back inside for a bit." I scramble to my feet, throwing my things back into my tote.

"We're not supposed to have those until we're thirty. Is it something I said? I'm sorry. I'll stop pushing." I don't mind Jess's endless boy talk. I'm just running from one boy in particular.

"No, you're fine," I insist. "I really just don't feel great. I'm going to lie down for a bit, so I'm ready to go for tonight. Bring home anyone you think is marriage material," I throw the joke over my shoulder as I walk as fast as possible without looking like I'm running for my life. It's hard to make an impressive getaway across the sand.

When I reach the side of the house, I turn back for an instant.

Bennett Sorenson's glare bores holes into me from across the beach. It's a challenge to catch my breath. He had always been the sun to me, filling my life with light. Looking at him now, there's none of that warmth. He's a shark, and I am the unsuspecting fish about to be his next meal.

I do exactly what he said I'm best at: run away.

At least I'm in my favorite swimsuit, not the t-shirt and sweats uniform I'd been planning for the week.

I stabilize myself against the wall. I can't feel my legs, I'm not sure how they've carried me this far.

Instead of going inside to wallow in self-pity, I zip up my hoodie and do a lap around the neighborhood. I need some distance from the beach. I need to be far from this entire town.

No matter where I go, every square mile of Harriettesville is encased in memories of us. Seeing Bennett has flipped some switch, letting the floodgates lower. I feel like a teenager again, overwhelmed by his presence. Before spotting him, I had almost convinced myself that I could play pretend for the week.

I stop by Books bookstore, searching for used mysteries and thrillers. Out of everywhere in town, this used to be my place. Bennett would join me sometimes, but I was usually alone while I wandered the ancient, towering shelves.

I soak in the smell of worn paper as I drift through the constant halo of dust that hangs in the shop. A fluffy, orange shop cat twirls through my legs as I read descriptions, making sure I don't pick up something I've already read. I see familiar titles. It's possible that they're the books I donated in the move, yet to find a new home.

The index cards I had placed years ago are still marking each section. They have yellowed and faded from the decay of time and humid, salt air. Just another reminder that even if I buried this place, it never forgot me.

I leave with enough books to spend the rest of the week in a corner reading. I'm back to my original plan.

The guys made certain that half the fridge is packed with beer. Right now is the perfect moment to take advantage of this. I crack open a can, curl up on the couch, and open the well-loved pages of the first novel in my new collection. It's about a private detective hired to solve a series of 'seemingly unrelated' crimes in Montana.

There are two ways to read a mystery. The first is to look closely at the breadcrumbs the author left behind and play Detective. But I'm a fan of the second way: to be swept away and surprised at every twist and reveal. It's been too long since I've read for fun, and it's surprisingly easy to sink into the familiar feeling of slipping away. For glorious hours, I'm not Emma, a girl running from her past. Instead, I'm Detective Hewitt, finding family heirlooms and severed limbs. As I approach the final chapter, where Detective Hewitt is setting up a grand reveal about how he solved the crimes, the back door slides open.

Jess walks in, followed by my worst nightmare. "I met these guys after you ran off. I wish you could have stayed longer, but I hope you're better now. They're on break from law school in Chicago. This is Ben. He said he lives next door, in the pink house. Isn't that crazy? And this is Jordan and Theo."

Jess doesn't know she is an absolute traitor welcoming the enemy into our sanctuary. When I told her to bring people home, I hadn't meant literally. Jess also doesn't know that when she places her hand on Bennett's arm, I want to punch her in the jaw.

"Actually, it's Bennett," he corrects. "Sorry you were feeling off earlier." His eyes narrow with suspicion while his words drip with concern.

"That's cool. Just a headache, but I might head to bed early tonight. It feels like it's coming back," I nod and stare intently at the page. What's the appropriate amount of time to fake read a page? One minute? Two? I glance up to see Bennett's gaze shift to the same kitchen cabinet door I had inspected yesterday.

"Come on, Emma. I have extra strength painkillers, and tonight will be so much fun." She turns to the guys, "We're going to do a game night and grill. You guys should totally join."

"Yeah, Emma, we wouldn't want you to miss out on any of the fun," Bennett says. Hearing my name on his lips for the first time in years sounds wrong, unfamiliar. There's no hint of joy or laughter that I'd come to know in his voice.

"Sounds great, but I don't think we have enough burgers," I murmur from the couch. It's my last attempt to dissuade them from joining. It's logical enough. We can't offer food we don't have.

Just yesterday, I was mourning this last spring break. Now, I'm ready to hide away.

No.

I'm not going to show I gave a damn. Or at least, any more damns because Bennett is not giving me the luxury of forgetting my escape on the beach.

"We can swing by my place to grab some extras. My family stays stocked. Sounds like the perfect night." Even after four years, Bennett always has the perfect solution, even if it's as simple as heading next door. He gives Jess one of his most impressive smirks.

Is he flirting with her?

He is absolutely trying to make me regret ever stepping back on that beach. Great. Maybe I should call Jackson and see if I can join him and his new girl at the cabin.

The guys return half an hour later with enough burgers to feed the entire neighborhood. The smell of the grill curls through the air, officially marking the end of our first full day in Harriettesville. At some point, before he had started flipping burgers, Caleb put on his cowboy hat. The combination of the grill, his hat, and the cheesy apron makes him look right at home. Our toppings are untraditional but an accumulation of who we are. Libby's homemade kimchi and Jess's white barbeque sauce that they brought in a cooler from Haven, and the slices of pineapple the guys had got for me on their grocery run.

We have to pull extra chairs out from inside for everyone to sit on.

By the time the food is ready, we're scrunched around the glass patio table with our loaded burgers, half of us using our laps because there's not enough room to set down our plates.

Bennett is so infuriatingly good at pretending we don't know each other. He asks everyone the types of questions you do when first meeting a group.

When he turns to me and asks, "What about you, Emma? Where are you from?" I choke on my bite of burger.

"She's from D.C.," Jess answers for me as I gulp down what I thought was my water, but is actually Josh's too strong mix of vodka and orange juice. The burn has me coughing.

"Oh, you must really like museums," he says, a wicked sparkle in his eyes. Who the hell is this, and where is my Bennett? The one that knows I hate that question.

"You must really like the beach," I reply, finally composed after my near-death by burger.

"What do you mean?"

"It feels pointless to assume someone likes the one thing everyone knows about where they live."

I must look crazy the rest of the night, looking at him longer than normal one minute and avoiding eye contact the next.

"We should play King's Cup," Caleb suggests, always the loudest advocate for games as a way to get more drunk.

"I'll go find the cards." I get up. Hunting down cards is the perfect opportunity to escape and collect my thoughts, even for a moment.

"I'll help." Bennett leaps up to join.

Who needs two people to find a deck of cards?

Before I can protest, Jess says, "That sounds like a great idea." She gives a knowing look, and Libby wiggles her eyebrows. Even though Jess flirted with him earlier, all is fair in love and beach trips. My friends are terrible at reading the room. Saying something now will make a scene, and I'm already so exhausted.

We head upstairs to the room I'm sharing with Jess.

"This was your parents' room, right?" He's the first to speak.

I hate that we're the only two people who know that. He also knows that my mom would have hated the new design. She would call the fake vintage travel posters 'forced' and make some comment about the comforter clashing with the pillowcases.

"Yeah." I start rummaging through my bags, avoiding looking back at him. I always keep an emergency pack of cards. A habit we had created together for rainy days or when one of us got tired of reading at the beach.

"What are you doing here?" He demands. That's the question I've been bracing for.

"I'm looking for cards. Isn't that the same reason you're up here?" I deflect.

"You know that's not what I mean," he grinds his teeth. "What are you doing here, in this house?"

"We're on spring break, just like you and your friends."

"Emma," he growls.

"It wasn't my choice. It was an accident," I concede. I don't feel like drawing this out anymore. It's draining, sparring with him, being someone that he hates. Or worse, someone he can be in the same room with without feeling the constant hum of electricity. I feel it, but he's freezing me out.

"Ok, then explain to me how ending up in your old house during spring break with a group of people who are obviously your friends is an accident?"

"Do you own the entire beach now?" I snap.

"No, but this all seems very convenient."

"And I was supposed to know you'd bring your friends here on spring break? It's not like we have a shared calendar to compare notes."

"You said you were never coming back. I just expected you to follow through on that." When I look into his eyes, I see my own feelings reflected back at me. Tears I didn't know I'd been holding back start to spill over. I didn't cry over Jackson, but this shatters me. He doesn't want here. I don't belong.

"It's not like that," I tell him everything. I tell him about finding Jackson with that girl, the drunk night out, and how some supernatural powers must have conspired to bring me here. It feels so normal, telling him everything, pouring out my heart, and not feeling embarrassed when I stumble over tear choked words. My throat is tight as I release a blubbering sound, "I wouldn't have come if I had known. I wouldn't have done that to you." I don't say that I wouldn't have done that to myself, either.

"I'm sorry," he stammers. I doubt he was prepared for this when he followed me. "I know with what happened with your parents-"

"I'm fine," I cut him off. "Well, not fine, but it's for the best. I'll leave if that's what you want. But the fact that you are here in my house again doesn't really make me think that's what you want. I think you want me to feel like shit every time I see your face." I've been enjoying spending time with my friends and even started believing that I could avoid the sticky emotions of being here. Now, I am willing to pack up and run.

Running is easier than facing this head on.

"This isn't your house anymore." He's right, and even though I just spilled my guts, we can't ignore reality.

"You know what I mean. I'm here, and you chose to be here. Jess didn't exactly drag you through that door."

"When I first saw you last night, I thought I was drunk out of my mind. Then today, I assumed you had come back under different circumstances."

"You saw me?"

He moves forward until his chest is inches from mine. His thumb brushes away the rouge tears still falling on my cheeks.

Up close, I can pick out the small changes. His shoulders are broader, and there's a permanent crease between his brows. His eyes now make me think of whiskey instead of honey. I could get drunk swimming in their burning depths if I'm not careful.

I'm the first one to pull away. I can't trust the heat in my chest or the way my fingers long to be tangled in his hair.

"Can we just be normal?" I plead, trying to put more than just physical distance between us. "I feel like I've screwed this trip up enough for them without throwing us into the mix. We can just keep pretending this is the first time we've met."

"Ok." His lips twitch like he wants to say something else but thinks better of it.

That self-destructive part of me wants him to say more. Something like *No, Emma. I could never pretend something like that.* But there's no use in acting like the conversation downstairs didn't happen.

This place makes me a daydreamer, calling up alternate realities that will never happen.

He stretches out his hand, and I take his pinkie in mine. Just like old times. The small act makes me want to let loose another round of tears, but it's not the time for that. Normal means no more crying. Normal means there is no reason I should want to cry each time I see him.

Jackson had been my longest relationship, but I've belonged to Bennett longer than anyone else. I just have to convince my body to remember we no longer belong to each other. We've agreed on normal, whatever normal is now. I have no doubts he can do it, but I'm not feeling that strong.

My eyes are still puffy from crying when we return to the group. Libby's face flashes with concern, but I shake my head. *Everything is fine.*

The drinking games ensure that everyone crosses the line from being tipsy to drunk. I'm religiously drinking water to avoid repeating yesterday's painful events. Still, I use my drink as an excuse not to talk. Each time I want to open my mouth, I take a sip instead. My own private game.

"I think it's time for Never Have I Ever!" Amber announces in a sing-song voice. She loves the game, especially when she's feeling drunk and nosey.

I'm expecting some form of protest from the rest of the group. I think I heard them playing on the ride over. We know everything about each other already, and it becomes largely a game of targeting whoever has had the most recent embarrassing exploits.

"I think it's a perfect idea," Jess leans into Bennett.

After we came downstairs, she asked what took so long, and I told her part of the truth: the cards were in a really inconvenient spot. She takes this to mean go for it because I didn't stake my claim.

"I'll go first! Never have I ever hooked up with a stranger on vacation," Jess says to which Josh, Jess, and both of Bennett's friends drink. No one calls her out for drinking on her own turn. It's obvious what game she's playing. Jess is many things, but subtle will never make the list.

"Never have I ever gotten a tattoo," I add for my turn, my go-to. When Bennett takes a sip, I barely restrain myself from breaking the Act Normal Deal we've just made. A stranger wouldn't know that he is deathly scared of needles.

"Never have I ever had a relationship longer than one year." It's Amber's attempt to get me to drink and another not so sly reminder it's time to find a new bed to jump into.

"This guy was not built for long term relationships. He breaks up with whoever he's seeing before he comes home,"

THE SUMMERS WE LEFT BEHIND

Theo nudges Bennett, who takes much more than the sip the game calls for.

"I really liked Casey. Why'd you have to go and dump him before the trip?" Jordan whines.

"It just wasn't working out. But thanks for the support, guys." He shoots his friends a look.

"It's a good thing we live in a big city. He's run through over half of our class by now," Theo jumps back in. I guess something that our friends have in common is that they don't quit while they're ahead.

I had done the same thing for a while. I met guys that seemed like Bennett in college. They had that same tousled look and easy smile, but they were nothing like him. They'd overexplain and be condescending when I just needed them to listen.

Jess had pointed out my type so easily earlier because I had run through so many Bennett look-a-likes. I had chased the feeling of him for almost two years.

Until Jackson. Jackson was straightforward and never had much going on below the surface. He was charming in a direct way that never left me guessing. Overnight, I swapped boys with unruly curls for groomed, simple perfection.

"Emma was totally the same way. We couldn't go to a bar without running into one of her hookups. Well, then there was Jackson," as the name slips from her lips, Jess looks shocked at her own words. "Shit, sorry. I didn't mean to."

"It's fine, Jess. I swear," I try to sound comforting. But I'm not looking at Jess. My gaze shifts to see Bennett's eyes flash with emotion.

So, what? He can sleep with whoever he wants, but I can't? Neither of us has a claim over the other anymore.

"Never have I ever done a walk of shame in my Halloween costume," Theo takes his turn, breaking up the awkwardness.

"The tights looked great on you the next day," Jordan snorts as Bennett drinks. At one point, I would have paid good money to have a picture of that costume.

"Never have I ever hooked up in the library," Libby says with a pointed glare at Amber and Josh, who both drink.

"It was only one time," Amber retorts.

"One time doesn't make me any less scarred." Libby is still bitter about walking in on them when they were supposed all be studying together. "I still have nightmares about it."

We continue to go around the circle until we are going out of turn, speaking up whenever someone thinks of something new. Everyone besides Caleb has had to refill their drink. He's always been the least scandalous.

"Never have I ever gotten stuck in a revolving door," Caleb says, looking at Jess, recalling the first and last time we visited Haven's Natural History Museum.

"Hey, they said it was broken. It wasn't my fault," Jess pouts.

"Never have I ever gone on a date with a professional athlete," Amber blurts out. I take a sip. She always brings this up when we're around new people. I don't blame her. It's a good story.

At the interested looks of Theo and Jordan, I give in, "He was a hockey player in town visiting family, and we met at a bar. We got dinner. Nothing happened. Just good conversation." It's not the version that Amber was hoping for. The one where he convinced me to go out with him by winning at darts. How the kiss at the end of the night left me dizzy. How we texted for a few months, and he even offered to fly me out to one of his games. Even if I wanted to, I can't seem to summon the words.

"Never have I ever hooked up on the beach," Caleb targets me. But I know that it applies to at least two of us. I take a long drink, trying not to look at Bennett.

"Oh my God, it was totally at this beach!" Libby is buzzing from figuring it out like she's about to win a prize for connecting the dots.

"Yeah, it was," I say, intently inspecting the contents of my cup.

"That's crazy. Bennett and you have so much in common." Jordan adds, tipping the balance for the realization I've hoped no one would have. I look around the room and see the dominos slowly start to fall.

"I guess everyone here just has sex on the beach. He told us that the girl used to be his neighbor," Theo says, continuing to paint a picture I'm intimately familiar with.

"Emma might know her. What was her name?" Jess jumps in.

"She is no one," Bennett adds quickly. His words twist in my gut as they hit home.

Libby doesn't miss the exchange between us. She gives me a *We'll talk later* look.

"Where did you live in town, Emma?" We had been skirting around the question, but now Bennett drops it right into my lap. He inclines his head. *What are you going to tell them?* So, his definition of 'normal' means pushing me to lie to my friends or admit the truth I've been desperately avoiding.

"Yeah, you never told us. It'd be fun to drive by and see the place you spent your summers," Jess says.

I'm not going to let him win this round. I was a coward then, but not anymore.

"We might be sitting in my old living room right now." I blush, but I want to strike back. I turn my attention to Bennett. "You didn't seem to recognize me, so I didn't want to bring it up. It must have not meant that much."

"Shit. You're the neighbor," Jordan whistles. I don't miss the look that passes between him and Theo. What has Bennett told them?

"I thought you looked like someone I used to know. You never texted back," Bennett's tone is cool and measured.

No one. Someone I used to know. The words continue to rattle through me.

The plan to be normal lasted all of one hour.

We've dealt our blows, and he's won. I shouldn't be surprised; he was always good at winning our stupid games.

Jess inches away from Bennett.

I get up to find another drink.

I take my time inspecting the options in the fridge and even consider the bottle of warm vodka on the counter. I had planned on taking it slow tonight, but if I take a shot or two, maybe I won't have to remember the dumpster fire of a day this has been so far.

"They really didn't know." Bennett sneaks up behind me. Could he just stop fucking doing that? Showing up. Following me.

"So, you decided to be an ass just in case they were in on it? You sound so surprised. Do you think I'm a liar now? That I orchestrated this entire thing?" I whisper yell to keep the conversation from carrying to the group. The moment upstairs had given me too much hope that we could be civil.

"No. I mean, I thought you might have maybe said something. I just don't know. It makes so much sense that you're here." *It just makes sense that I would come back.*

"You know what else would make sense? You leaving us alone."

"Why would I do that when I'm starting to have so much fun?" He turns, leaving me standing there.

Our spat at least gives me some valuable information. I'm not the only one navigating an obstacle course of emotions. But he's not finished making me miserable.

When I return, tension hangs thick in the air, affecting everyone except for Josh and Amber, who are about five minutes away from taking advantage of their shared room. The group has switched to some form of Simon Says, involving way more alcohol than the last time I played it in elementary school.

There are no more flashback-inducing incidents throughout the night. As the guys head back to the Pink House, I can't help but release a breath.

It's over, for now.

I'm brushing my teeth when Libby finds me. "Why didn't you say something."

"It's just easier not to talk about it. It's not like I really know him anymore. Like he said, we're strangers." The word stings as it passes my lips. Bennett and I were never really strangers. We were in each other's lives from the first time we met. It's weird to become something we never were to begin with.

"Easier to not talk about your hot ex-neighbor who you hooked up with one time?" I wince at how stupid it sounds. I thought I had escaped the interrogation portion of the night.

But I haven't ever told them much about Bennett except for the basics. And those basics never included a name. I had once told them the messy and uncomfortable reality of hooking up on the beach. All they knew was one awkward party story. One story will never be enough to explain what he means- what he meant to me.

"It wasn't just one time. We really fucked each other up." I explain my four summers in Harriettesville. How a summer boy became my first love and first heartbreak. How I cried to Cammie and Corrina. How I almost never went to Haven.

"Em, if you told us, I would have personally made sure his ass never stepped foot on the property. And I can't believe your sister, who you only talk to once a year, knows, but you didn't tell your best friends." I can tell that part hurts her. Corrina seems like a shit sister to anyone outside our relationship, but we show up when we need each other. No questions asked.

"Thank you, and I'm sorry, but it's easier to forget it. I never expected to be here again. And I didn't want to cause more drama after the Jackson thing. This is your vacation, and I just crashed it."

"The fact that you're calling your long-term boyfriend cheating on you a 'thing' is as wild as thinking we wouldn't want you to be comfortable. We're all just happy you're here for one last trip." She gives me one of those hugs that reminds me of being wrapped up in a blanket. I usually hate hugs, but I love Libby hugs.

"Honestly, we talked it out, and it's fine. It's just weird. Like I jumped in a time machine or stepped into another universe." I mean it. I was mad at first that he inserted himself into our plans, and there's no way that things will be normal, but I'll deal.

"As long as you're sure. The guys are fun, but you're more important," she shrugs. "It does seem like a sign from the universe. Like the fact that you're back in this same place."

"The universe must hate me for it to take my boyfriend cheating on me to get me here," I laugh. The two things she checks first in the morning are the weather and her horoscope.

"Or it saved you from being the future Mrs. Jackson Mathews." Libby has always been the number one Jackson hater. She claims he dimmed my sparkle. "You better go talk to Jess. She's drunk and stressed that you'll never speak to her again." Libby leaves the bathroom and heads downstairs.

I comfort Jess, letting her know everything is cool between me and Bennett. How was she supposed to know that he was the ghost of summers' past?

I sweat through the night, haunted by my happiest years.

5

Summer

Seven years ago

I come prepared to capture every instant this summer. I snag a dual pack of disposable cameras at one of our gas station stops. I know one won't be enough.

May had stretched so long that I could barely stand waiting. I packed my bag weeks ago, this time feeling like an expert in proper beach attire.

After the necessary ritual of unloading groceries and luggage, I run over to the Pink House. I know Bennett is already inside, waiting for me. Once I told him we were on the way, every few minutes, he would text *how much longer?* I love that he's as anxious to see me as I am to see him.

The front door to the Pink House is unlocked, so I let myself in. I find Diane, Tanner, and Bennett in the dining area playing cards. The sound of a local radio station playing throwback hits flows through the room.

"You didn't text when you got to town," Bennett complains after he hugs me.

"I just wanted to keep you on your toes," I say. It wasn't intentional. I was just in such a rush I forgot to send anything.

"We literally had to drag him away from waiting at the window," Tanner informs me.

I sit down and join them, the card game now abandoned for the sake of catching up. From what I can tell, Tanner was winning. I've never seen him lose.

"I can't believe you're done with your first year of high school. It feels like you were just a kid the last time I saw you," Diane says, sounding so proud of me. Like I did something impossible instead of something millions of teenagers do each year.

"Mom, you literally met her last year. Isn't that a bit dramatic?" Tanner asks.

"What's life without a little drama?" She turns her attention back to me, "Speaking of drama, how was Homecoming? Please tell me you went with someone and have pictures. This is why I always wanted daughters." I pull out my phone and find the picture I like best of me and Henry. My dress was layers of light pink ruffles that made me feel like a rose.

"We're literally right here." Bennett waves his hand in front of Diane's face to make sure she can see him.

Tanner watches the three of us with rapt attention from where he's scarfing ice cream on the couch.

"Hush," Diane waves his words away. "You look so good in that dress. And your date, he's cute. What's he like?" Henry is cute. He has long lashes that I'd obsessed over that entire night and ocean blue eyes that were the reason he convinced me to go with him in the first place. Diane's excited reaction, even though months after the actual dance, makes the event feel complete.

"He's nice, I guess. He's a sophomore and has a car, which was cool." I don't know why I feel awkward talking about another boy here.

"Bennett went to his first Homecoming too. He couldn't last year because he caught pneumonia. His date had a beautiful dress, but yours is much more elegant." She pulls up a photo on her phone. I love the girl's dress. It's a cascade of little hearts that hovers just above her knees. But I can't shake the unease I felt seeing Bennett's arm wrapped around her waist.

"What's she like?" I ask.

"Umm, she's nice." Bennett pauses, then adds, "We went with a big group."

"Do you guys have any other words to describe people?" Tanner finally pipes in, "I doubt everyone is nice."

We continue to pick apart the last year.

"What about you? Aren't you supposed to be applying for college or something?" I drag Tanner in from the sidelines.

"Applications aren't due until December," He glares at me.

"Oh, so you don't have a plan."

"I'm going to study math," he says proudly. He's so serious. I can't help but blink at him in confusion. It's so unlike him. Bennett has always seemed like the smart brother. Tanner just floated through life. I always thought he was like me, just happy to end up somewhere.

"Math? Isn't that hard?" I don't mean to sound insulting, but that's how it comes out.

"I'm good with numbers," he shrugs, brushes off my rudeness, and shifts back to his casual demeanor, popping another spoon full of ice cream into his mouth.

Before I can continue to make a fool of myself, Richard pushes through the door, arms loaded up with groceries. "I heard we have a special guest for dinner. I couldn't help but pick up something." He begins to unload the bags, revealing the ingredients for pesto gnocchi, my favorite meal from last summer.

I jump up to help, but he insists I relax after the long drive. As we wait for dinner to be ready, Bennett and I make Diane personal social media accounts so we can stay connected.

We carry the meal outside once it's finished. Even though we're all gathered together, Diane still blows her conch shell horn as if asking the rest of the neighborhood if they want to join. As the sun sets, casting a golden glow on the horizon, I know there is no place I'd rather be.

It isn't until we're headed off to sleep that I return home. Days like these make me want to stay and sleep on the couch, knowing I'll just be back tomorrow.

Everything in the Sorenson house has a purpose. I don't mean a purpose like it brings out the blue in the accent pillows, or it fills up the empty white space in the corner. No, the cute little sea turtle in the kitchen is also a timer. If it isn't something you can use, it captures a memory. There is a jar of sand that Diane and Richard had brought with them on their honeymoon, collecting little bits from every beach they visited in France and Spain.

That's why I'm excited when I spot the record player in the corner. The setup wasn't here last summer. My eyes skim the stacks to find albums and artists I know. I've never used one before, and they wouldn't have it out unless it's meant to be enjoyed. I want to listen as the needle dances across a record.

"Can we use it?" Even though I know the answer, I'm scared to touch it without invitation.

"Why else would we have it out?" Bennett smiles as he watches my excitement grow.

On one of the few occasions I've gone to a school friend's house, I'd asked the same question, and they had given me an entire speech about the value of collectibles. He went on and on about 'how sometimes things are more valuable when you don't use them.' That still seems pointless to me.

I sit down and immediately start searching through the options. "What do you listen to?" Is he a classic rock guy? Or maybe bluegrass? We've never just sat and shared music before. It's one of the things I haven't discovered about him yet. Before long, there's a growing stack of records beside me.

"What about we each pick one album?" He loves little games like this. As if he's adopted the trait from the things in his home, his questions are more than questions. I know what to pick the moment I catch a glimpse of its blue cover. I tuck the record behind my back and wait for him to make a selection.

"Ready?" I ask, excited to learn more about the boy across from me. "One, two, three."

I pull out ABBA's *Voulez-Vous* while he holds *Born in the U.S.A.*.

"I've never listened to Springsteen," I admit.

"Well, then, it's about time you get educated. It's essential if you're going to be here for the Fourth."

Ever since Diane's birthday last year, they have given me a no questions asked invitation to every party or event that is in any way Sorenson adjacent. Missing last year's Fourth celebrations has only made me more excited to join this year.

My family will be in town, too, because my mother wants to avoid making the drive, and she's convinced Dad and Corrina to come out for the holiday weekend.

Bennett sets it up the sound system, carefully placing the needle in the groove as I watch from the floor. Watching Bennett has quickly become one of my favorite summer hobbies. The speakers blast sound in the sweet spot between too loud and just loud enough to fill every corner of the room. He spins around when the lyrics of "Born in the

U.S.A." start, pretending to hold a microphone and singing along.

With anyone else, the comedic scene would make me cringe with secondhand embarrassment. But the only thing I want to do is preserve this moment. I pull the disposable camera from my back pocket. Once the camera clicks, he snatches it and holds it up to his face to take one of me.

When he's done, he asks, "Do they make copies of film pictures, or is it just one and done? Cause I want some too." I have no idea. This is my first time using a disposable camera. But they have to be able to make multiple if you ask?

"I'm not sure. But you could get a camera too." I've thought of giving him my extra one.

"No, they're more special when you take them. Also, I never know when the right moments are."

This is the moment I start to fall hopelessly for Bennett Sorenson. Each moment before this was just a sprinkle of affection building to the wave that now threatens to pull me under.

The Fourth of July has always been a stuffy event. Our family would go to some catered barbeque disguised as family fun, but it was really just a work event or fundraiser. Anyone under seventeen would be at the same table, and the high schoolers would pass around a flask and gossip. We were expected to dress up, not a swimsuit in sight. Without fail, I would stain the white dress my mom bought me for the occasion.

Now, I get to wear cut offs and a T-shirt with a bikini underneath. If I spill a drink all over myself, I can run into the ocean.

When Diane caught wind that my entire family would be in town, she jumped on the opportunity to have everyone over. She's never met my dad. He ended up never coming to the house last year. Corrina is also flying out from her law internship in New York.

When we arrive, I'm embarrassed for my family for the first time in my life. Despite telling them it was a casual dinner, my mother and Corinna are both in dresses and hedges so thin that they sink into the sand as they cross the beach. Dad is only slightly better in a polo shirt and chinos. Tanner and Bennett are in their swimsuits, like me. Diane looks flawless in a flowing, wrap coverup over her own swimwear. Here I am the one that fits in.

Smoke is already drifting up from the grill. American flags are scattered everywhere, with red, white, and blue paper plates on the table to match the theme.

Bennett was right about the music. In addition to the sizzling of burgers, the outdoor speaker system blasts oldies with a particularly heavy rotation of Springsteen hits.

"Hey, kid." Tanner ruffles my hair right before Bennett picks me up to spin me around. I squeak as he squeezes me so tight the breath rushes out of me.

"I'm fifteen now, asshole! Stop calling me kid." I resist the urge to flip off Tanner.

"Emma Claire," my mother scolds at the casual exchange. Tanner has started to become the older brother I've never had. Each of his taunts makes me more confident to throw back a retort. Now they come as easily as breathing.

Tanner and Bennett exchange a look and mouth, *Emma Claire*. It dawns on me. They haven't heard my double name before.

"We are in charge of the fireworks this year. Hope you're not scared." Bennett whispers in my ear. Yes, I am a little scared. I'm anxious about anything that could go wrong. Last year, I'd only seen them from a distance.

I look over to see that the third Sorenson brother is transfixed by my sister. They're the same age but live opposite lives. Jones is working in civil engineering and is as smart as my sister, but his job involves dusty construction sites. I only met him a couple of times last summer. He is the softest spoken Sorenson with features less hard and striking than his brothers.

Corrina is polished and always buried in books or whatever posh asshole has caught her eye. From her platinum shoulder length hair to the designer sandals, it's obvious that she was born to be in the city.

Having my family flood in makes me oddly protective of these people I've only known for a year yet have come to love so dearly. My dad is talking to Richard, who expertly redirects the flow of conversation away from work. Richard works long hours through the summer in the mayor's office, assisting with the tourist season. He has a strict policy of no work talk at home, which he tries to hold Diane to as well, but she loves the café so much she can't help but talk about it.

"Everyone that wants cheese on their burger, raise your hand," Richard calls out, slapping down slices of cheddar on the patties. I know they have pineapple slices set aside for me. When I told them about pineapple on burgers, they had no idea what I was talking about.

Now Tanner and I both insist it's an essential topping. This is where being comfortable is the default more than an option. My parents brought a bottle of wine that looks out of place on the table with the spread of chips and beer.

The conversation throughout dinner stays stiff and too formal. No one seems to ask the right questions. I was being too optimistic, thinking our families would mesh.

With full stomachs and a darkening sky, Tanner, Bennett, and I escape toward the beach. Other groups are already clustered with their own impressive stashes of rockets. The air is filled with sizzling cracks and pops from the explosions.

"Ladies first." Tanner has set up the first firework and is now presenting me with the lighter like it is a magical sword.

I light the fuse. It's too late to worry about the combustive power that I am wielding, but I still do. Plenty of people get into accidents with these things every year.

I back up until I hit something solid, or in this case, someone.

I look behind me and see Bennett. When our eyes collide, I register that he is holding me steady with firm hands on my waist. Hands that haven't let go despite the fact I've caught my balance. The loud crackling of the firework jerks us apart. I can still feel the lingering presence of his fingers pressing against my sides.

"God, Emma, it's not going to bite you, and it's pointed in the opposite direction. If you do accidentally catch on fire, I'll be happy to toss you into the ocean," Tanner calls out at my reaction. "Shit, the lighter's out." He shakes the lighter one last time, attempting to get it to work.

"I thought you grabbed the new ones we bought," Bennett says.

"I guess not." Tanner now holds the lighter to his ear like it will tell him its secrets.

"I can grab another from the house. I want water anyway." I still feel hot from the brief contact. Am I reading too much into that one moment?

I run back up the beach. As I'm about to step into the light cast from the house, I notice two figures in the sand. The bleached hair of the girl nearly glows in the dark. Straddling her is someone who is undeniably a Sorenson.

Jones.

The only one that isn't down on the beach. They don't see me.

I want to pull them apart and scream at my sister. Why would she do this? How could she take a single day and make it so complicated?

I don't do anything. I won't give her the satisfaction.

I want to scrub the image of them from my mind. I had said I wanted our families to get along, but this was on another level. More importantly, I don't trust Corrina.

After grabbing the lighter, I come back from the opposite side of the house.

I don't tell the guys when I get back to the beach.

I won't ruin this.

Instead, I have a smile plastered on my face as I hand off the lighter to Tanner. An expression that is supposed to say, *Everything is perfectly fine. I didn't just see our siblings going at it.*

"You ok? You look tense," Bennett leans in, concerned.

"I'm good. It's just the fireworks. I don't think I'll ever get used to being this close." It's the first lie I've told him. The words feel caustic on my tongue. I'm relieved that the lies don't come easily. The pit in my stomach is enough to never want to do it again.

No matter how hard I try, it's hard to appreciate the rest of the night.

The unease and confusion follow me to bed, where I spend most of the night staring at the ceiling.

The next morning, Corrina is already fully dressed and sipping coffee when I come downstairs.

"How was your night?" I ask, giving her this one chance to say something.

"Uneventful. I am surprised that there were no fires with all the contraband everyone was setting off."

"You're messing with me, right? What were you thinking? Hooking up with my best friend's brother."

"I thought Cammie was your best friend?" She deflects. "And what does it even matter? I'm leaving tonight. He was fine, but any townie who thinks they have a long term shot with either of us is delusional." She is always so dismissive of people and opportunities. There will always be another option for her, so why care about the one she already has?

"I can't believe you said that," I spit out. "These people mean something to me, and you took that for granted." Fresh hot rage fills me. They invited her into their home. These people hold a deep precious part of me, and she still feels like she can say that.

"You'll learn that guys like your Sorenson boys don't stay in your life forever. But have fun in the meantime." She flicks her platinum bob and walks out to the deck. I avoid her the rest of the day. No words that might pass between us can help.

I'm more than happy to get my family back on the road and out of town. I even help pack up the bags to get them out faster. Still, Corrina's venom haunts me for days. It's like a slow acting poison flowing into the crevices of my mind. We had always traded verbal blows, but few had ever cut this deep. When the words resurface, I can only think about the possibility that I don't belong here after all.

Do the Sorensons see it too? Will they see the infectious grey cloud that hovers over my family and politely ask me to leave them alone? The knot keeps tightening in my stomach. What hits me hardest is the possibility that this might be temporary.

Two days after the Fourth, I'm waiting for Bennett on the swing. We're back to our pre-holiday routine. He's working longer today because some other employees are out of town. I nearly get through an entire book before he steps out to find me.

"I saw Jones hooking up with my sister on the beach during the Fourth." The words fly out of my mouth before I lose my nerve. I've been keeping what I had seen to myself and felt like I was about to burst open from hiding it for so long.

"Why didn't you say something."

"I'm saying something now."

"You waited days when you could've said something right after."

"I didn't know how to say it." Correction. I hadn't known how to say it without blowing up an entire evening that had already been rocky.

"That's why you were so tense," he realizes. I don't deny it. "I asked, and you chose to hide this." I've never seen him this close to anger before. He storms away before I can apologize. I go to Early Bird the next day, but he's not there.

It's the loneliest I've ever felt at the beach.

For the first time this summer, I call Cammie. We are now definitively more than school friends, but I've never needed advice like this before.

"Ok. So, first of all, your sister is a raging bitch. He has a right to be upset, but at the same time, you need to process it first. Seeing a family member doing shit like that is horrific. I would have gone non-verbal if I was you." Her words take a weight off my chest.

"What do I do."

"Give him a few days, then apologize."

"Apologize for what? You just said what I did makes sense."

"He's hurt. Set some boundaries, communicate."

"Thanks for picking up."

"Thanks for the drama. I've literally been watching paint dry. It's some sort of performance art piece my parents dragged me to. You gave me an out."

"I miss you."

"Miss you too. Go fix things with your summer boy."

It's three days before I see him again, the longest we've spent without seeing each other during the summer. The distance made me aware of how scared I am to lose our friendship.

It's Saturday morning, and I wait for him to do his rounds to clean up the beach. I get up earlier than normal and sit on the porch until his backdoor slides open. The moment he's on the sand, I run after him. He's moving so quickly that I have to match his long strides.

"I'm sorry." I move in front of him so he can see that I mean what I'm saying. "I really didn't think. I shouldn't have hidden that from you."

"It's fine, but you're right. We don't lie to each other, Emma. I thought I could always rely on you to be honest, even if you think it's embarrassing. This was just such a big thing to hide. I want to still trust you, but I don't want to do this again. It hard fighting with you when all I want to do is tell you about the asshat at the coffee shop that ordered three poached eggs instead of just ordering like a normal person."

"Let's not fight anymore."

"I promise." He holds out his pinkie, and I take it.

Over the last month, my mind had wandered to thinking we could be more. We are still fragile and new in terms of friendships, and I can't risk letting these other feelings out if it means feeling like I have over the last three days. It means deceiving him again, keeping a part of me hidden.

But unlike what happened on the beach, I'll be the only one that knows.

Bennett is running late from his shift. I came to the Pink House to meet him. But the notification on my phone lets me know I'll be waiting another fifteen minutes. I hover over a cluster of frames. I'm always drawn to this corner with the picture of carefree newlyweds being captured in time.

"That one's also my favorite," Diane says, standing beside me. Seeing her and the picture side by side, I can tell she's never lost the sparkle in her eyes. If anything, now it's more blinding.

"How did you two meet?"

"We were at a party on the beach. Not this one, though. We both went to schools in California," It makes sense for Diane to always be near a beach. I can't imagine her anywhere else. "I was proving to some guy that I could pour the perfect beer. Which I did flawlessly. I didn't know Richard was watching. I guess I made an impression because later that night, he told me he was going to marry me. I told him he had quite a few dates to make up for before that would ever happen. The next day, we went to this terrible bar. Broken barstools and music that made me want to cut off my ears. He had just gotten a new beer when I told him I wanted to leave. He said he had to finish his beer first. I finished it for him when he got up to go to the bathroom. He didn't mind, so I asked him on a second date."

It's not the story I was expecting, but it's so true to who they are. I had asked my mother the same question once, and she just said that she and my father met through mutual friends.

"That's perfect," I say. The Sorensons are becoming my new definition of that word.

I had grown up thinking my family was perfect. Perfect in the way a staged house is. But when you pick an apple from the fruit bowl and take a bite, you realize it's plastic, and you figure out none of it is real. It's all a production.

Leaving a second time is easier. I survived last time, and I know I'll be back, that the magic of Harriettesville won't disappear in nine months.

After getting home, I rush to develop the pictures I had taken. I had run out of film and needed a third camera. I show them to Cammie. I didn't take good pictures on my phone last summer, and now I get to show her the beach and how it's supposed to be captured.

"You look different in these."

"Like more tan?"

"No, like more yourself. You're smiling in every picture."

"I smile plenty," I emphasize by throwing on a grin.

"Not like this, you don't. It's my mission to get a picture of you in the city looking like this. I like this version of you."

I like that version of me too. It's my favorite.

6
Monday
Now

I picked up running after we sold the summer house. It became a tool to combat the anxiety that floods through my system. So many things make me anxious these days. Thinking about the future and my parents' endless calls and questions about it are usually at the top of this list.

I wish that 'I don't know' could be the answer because that's all I can come up with. So many things in my life are blank spaces that I don't have the ability to fill.

After the horrors of last night, Bennett has taken the top spot.

Though drunk me had been a fairly impressive packer, ensuring I had real clothes and toiletries for the week, she hadn't grabbed running shoes. What I do find is the old Portland College hoodie that has been living in the farthest depths of my closet in an unpacked box. I throw it back in the duffle and head outside.

I've always wanted to run barefoot on the beach but haven't had the chance until now. Fifteen minutes in, and I'm already exhausted. The combination of running on sand and the not so healthy choices of the weekend are draining away my strength. I am by no means a track star, that's all Libby, but I expected to last longer before wanting to turn back and admit defeat.

I run into the ocean, embracing the water's icy bite, cooling my overheating skin. My tank top and shorts are soaked, sticking to my skin as I step back on land. I instantly regret my detour when a wind whips through, making the cool temperature frigid.

After a steaming hot shower, I head downstairs to retrieve the coffee Amber picked up from Early Bird.

Apparently, Bennett and I are expertly executing the act of being normal because no matter what activity we plan, he and his friends get a no questions asked invite to everything we do.

Theo mentioned last night that we can play volleyball now that there are nine of us, which is what we're now in the process of setting up. The Sorensons have a portable net that takes us half an hour to set up because Caleb and Jordan insist they can do it without help or instructions.

"You're doing great, guys. But that looks like it's set up for babies," Jess says when they somehow set it up upside down.

"Can you please put us out of our misery? This is starting to get painful," I ask Bennett.

"I'm enjoying the show. I'll set it up in ten minutes if they still haven't managed to figure it out." He's reclining on a towel, sipping from a water bottle. My eyes track a stray drop of water as it rolls off his chin, hitting his shirt.

When the net is finally in position, we split the teams. Theo stays to the side to play referee. Two guys and two girls on each side, so no one will have a height advantage. On my side, it's Caleb, Jordan, Jess, and me.

It's cathartic to direct my energy towards the game. My legs are shaky from running on the sand, but it's easy to regain energy when I picture the ball as Bennett's face and spike it hard over the net. We lock eyes after I make the first point. The air crackles between us, and he nods his head.

The message is clear.

Game on.

We don't lose intensity as we match each other point for point. The rest of the group is panting as they try to keep up with us. Josh and Libby are full on athletes, but Josh is distracted by Amber's shorts, and Libby has never been great at hand-eye coordination.

"Damn, guys. This isn't the Olympics," Jordan says to himself, returning one of Bennett's brutal spikes.

My focus finally snaps when Jess hits the ground a little too hard while scooping the ball. I see her getting up just as Bennett returns the ball.

Hard.

Right into my face.

Now I'm on the ground, and I can feel blood trickling down my face, but my nose is numb.

"Shit," Bennett says. He sprints over to me.

"This is what you guys get for acting like pros," Amber shouts from the other side of the net.

I see Bennett pull off his shirt and hold it to my face to stop the blood. I hate that even with my damaged face. I note how it smells like him. That smoke and wood smell touched with some new musky cologne is like a drug. The summer before my senior year of high school, he had given me one of his shirts to take home. I had worn it until it didn't smell like him anymore. Now it's in a box. A box in my room in Haven, tucked away with everything else I can't manage to throw away.

It hasn't been warm enough to justify going casually shirtless during the trip. The only other time I've seen him in just his swimsuit was from a distance. Now I drink in every well-defined inch of him. He had been fit at nineteen, but he's filled out. From my angle on the ground, he occupies my entire field of vision. I see a glimpse of the tattoo on the left side of his chest. I don't pick out what it is as a new wave of blood spews from my face.

"I think I'm going to head inside," my voice is nasal as I talk. I stand up to go.

"I'll come too," Bennett says.

"I think you've done enough," I shoot back. He looks worried, but why should I feel guilty? He's the one that made this happen in the first place.

Back in the house, the blood has stopped, but my nose has started throbbing. I wrap ice in a towel and hold it lightly against my face.

It only takes a few minutes for him to follow me inside.

"Can you not follow me?" I glare from behind the towel.

"I just wanted to make sure you were ok."

"I'm not your responsibility anymore. When I tell you to stop following me around, I mean it. I'm not secretly hoping you'll chase after me." I don't have to disguise my annoyance because it's just us. The pain only makes me want to lash out at him more; I don't care if he's just a convenient target.

He doesn't seem to register my irritation or demands, "This reminds me of that time-"

"Me too." I cut him off. I don't want him to bring the memories out in the open. They have been just beneath the surface, and saying them out loud is a form of acknowledgment that I don't want to deal with right now.

"I bet it looked like I was aiming for you, but I wasn't planning on breaking your face. I really like your face the way it is." Is he trying to compliment me right now? With blood on my shirt and a bruise forming?

"I hope I'm permanently deformed."

"Maybe that's what I need to help me stop staring at you."

"You haven't been staring at me."

"How do you know that?" Well, shit. How do I know he hasn't been staring at me? Maybe because my attention has been glued to him.

"I just do."

"Maybe I'm just better at hiding it than you." So, he has noticed.

"I'm just making sure you don't fuck up this trip any more than you already have."

"I've been a perfect gentleman. That can change if you want it to." His features turn devilish. "You're friends are pretty hot. You keep good company."

"You wouldn't." My eyes narrow. The movement sends a shot of pain through my nose, starting yet another bloody mess.

He laughs, "Jealous, Danes?"

"Just disappointed. You're starting to act like your dick of a brother." It's a low blow. The last time we discussed Tanner, it hadn't ended well. And Tanner was only a dick because that's what he wanted people to expect.

We're having an epic stare down when our friends come inside. Me, with blood all over me, and him, looking like a satisfied cat leaning against the counter.

"You feeling any better?" Amber asks.

"Yeah. It's not that bad. You guys didn't play another game?" They still could have with the seven of them.

"Nah, you bleeding everywhere kind of killed the vibe," Jordan says from the couch. We really are starting to be one large group.

Jess and Amber start dinner. They'd planned for seafood pasta and salad tonight. Bennett makes himself useful by chopping vegetables. I might not have minded that he was helping, but he kept casually grazing Jess's arm and feeding her little bits of the chopped vegetables for the salad.

I'm preparing the table outside when he comes out with a salad bowl overflowing with greens. By this point, I have already considered the collection of spaces in the house that would be perfect for hiding a body. It isn't just him touching someone else that makes me murderous. I also can't make sense of his fucked up game. I can't reconcile the boy I knew with the person next to me.

"You're still terrible at concealing your emotions," he says.

"I don't have any emotions to conceal." I adjust the placemat in front of me for the third time.

"Oh, so you just glare daggers at all the guests you have over. You must be a great hostess."

"Only the ones who act like my friends' emotions are things to play with. Cut. It. Out." I hope my words have the bite I intend.

"I will, but only because you asked so nicely." Fuck him. Fuck his hot and cold attitude. One second he's trying to take care of me, comforting me about Jackson and giving me his shirt for my bloody nose. The next, he turns into someone I don't know.

He stays true to his word and doesn't hit on Jess during dinner. Later that night, I can tell the damage is done.

"Would you mind if I hooked up with Bennett? We have this vibe going, but I would never touch him without talking to you first. I know it's been years, but still."

I'm washing my face, splashing water to hide whatever thoughts slip onto my features. "Go for it."

As long as he's not playing games with her to get to me, why not? He's not mine anymore. He hasn't been mine for four years. I need to get that through my head. It's time to put off letting him go.

"If that changes, promise you'll say something. You've always mattered more than any guy." As she says this, my jealousy melts. None of this is her fault. Maybe if they do get together, I can finally get it through my head that he and I are over. Hopefully, then my body won't crave him each time we're alone together.

"I love you." I mean it with every fiber of my being. I won't lose her over some boy that I knew four years ago. Even if that boy is Bennett.

"Love you too."

7
Tuesday
Now

After my morning run, I head to Early Bird. It's my turn in the rotation to go on a coffee run. I could go to the newer shop just another block away, but that would be a betrayal. I also know that if I tell them I can't handle going back, they'll let me off the hook.

I'm no coward.

I can get coffee by myself.

Unless she's finally hired a manager, Diane will be there. Did Bennett tell her that I'm back? In some ways, I am more scared to see her than I was to see him.

I had no real reason to cut her out of my life. Still, after I did, she kept trying to reach out over the years. She would send pictures and quotes that I couldn't look at for long before wanting to cry. She and Richard had shown me what life could look like: a home full of messy, wonderful love.

The bell above the door jingles as I push through. After a quick scan, I there are no Sorensons in sight. I can't tell if I'm relieved or disappointed. After placing an order for six drinks, I wait at the end of the bar, mindlessly tapping away on my phone.

A loud gasp has me looking up and turning toward the sound. Diane is carrying a crate of ingredients, wearing her flour dusted apron. She rushes in, drops the crate, and wraps me in her arms.

"My Emma. Oh, you're still so perfect." There are more laugh lines around her mouth and crinkling in the corner of her eyes. She once told me that she never minded them and that they are a reminder of living a good life. "Let me put these away, and I'll be right out."

Just then, the barista calls out my order. I could tell Diane that I'm in a hurry to get back and I'll come back later. But that would be a lie, and I've never lied to Diane. No matter how long I've avoided her, I won't start now. I've known this entire time that talking to her means saying the things out loud that I've been avoiding.

"Sure, I'll just go sit outside." I head for the swing, setting the drinks on the little table next to it. The cushions have been reupholstered. The thick waterproof fabric is now a watercolor style covered with ocean animals instead of the neon stripes they had been the last time I was here. It only takes a few moments for Diane to follow me out.

"It feels so right to see you sitting here. This porch felt so empty without you waiting and reading." She sits down next to me, handing me a cookie she's brought with her.

"I should have stopped by sooner. I've been in town for a couple of days now."

"I heard the boys come in last night talking about some neighbor girl that sounded an awful lot like you. It was easy to put things together." She winks, "I didn't want to spook you by popping over before you were ready. What happened to your face?" Bruises have bloomed around my nose, and because I came from my run, I didn't have the chance to cover it with makeup. Now that she's closer, she probably can see the tinges of blue.

"You're son doesn't know how to aim a volleyball." She winces on my behalf. "Honestly, the only reason I'm in town is because of a messy situation I was running away from." I look down at the cookie, too nervous to take a bite.

"I, for one, am a big supporter of messy situations that bring people back to where they belong."

"You're not mad at me?"

"Don't be silly. You've seen what my boys have done, and they still get invited back for Christmas every year. Tanner told me all about the fight when Bennett wouldn't. I told that boy he better beg for forgiveness more than he had ever begged for anything in his life if he wanted you back."

During the fallout, I never wanted Diane to take a side. They were family, I was just the girl next door that crashed into their lives. I loved them. I even thought I was one of them for brief, fleeting moments. Warmth fills my chest at her words, knowing that she fought for me, even when I pushed all of them away. Bennett did try, but I closed myself off so completely. I was the one who sealed our fate.

"That really means the world to me. I thought I blew it. Each time you sent a message, I thought so long about replying, then it felt like I waited too long."

"Eventually, you'll realize that four years isn't that long. Right now, that's how the phases of your life are measured four years in high school, then another four or more in college. Knowing you have time doesn't make it easier to miss someone, but it gives you hope." She squeezes me into a side hug. "There are people I haven't seen in a decade that I only talk to once a year, and I still love them. I'm just happy you came back before too long."

"He's so different."

"Did you expect him to be the same after everything?"

"No." It might have hurt more if he was fine. It would have felt like I was easy to wipe away.

"Give him time. Give yourself time, too," she tells me. I nod, but despite her words, I can't help but feel like time is running out. In a few days, I'll be miles away.

"I've missed you so much. I'm scared to ask, but did the cayenne dark chocolate muffins ever make it on the menu?"

"Yes, but people couldn't take the heat, so they didn't last long."

She shows me pictures of some of her new creations. The most unique is an avocado blueberry muffin; I mentally take pity on whoever had been selected to test out the flavor.

I only get up to leave when I see the coffees have started to sweat in their plastic cups. I give her one last hug. Maybe this is why I love Libby's hugs. They feel just like Diane's.

"You're still always welcome to come by the house when you're ready," she calls as I reach the last step.

"Thank you." One day, I promise myself. When Bennett and I are done with whatever war he's waging. I don't see it happening this week, but maybe one day when we're older. When we love other people, and I feel whole without him. I'll meet his children and love them because they have his features, even if they don't have mine.

After I deliver the coffee, we make our way through the tourist shops and boutiques. Most of the clothes are the same as what we could get anywhere else but buying things on vacation, connecting a memory with something you can wear back home, is special. If someone asks where you got it, you get to say, 'On vacation.'

"If I wasn't already going to New York this fall, I would move here and start my own shop," Jess says.

"This place wouldn't survive you," I joke.

Jess is the most dazzled by the experience, talking to shop owners and a few local designers. I can't imagine her lasting too long in a place as small as Harriettesville. She thrives on a constant flood of new people, and the tourists wouldn't suffice the same way they do for Diane.

"It really is special." Amber picks up a blue linen sundress from a display, running the fabric through her fingers. "Emma, why have you never talked about this place before? It's literally perfect." It had been perfect for me too. My little bubble away from reality. Libby hasn't told them everything, which is for the best.

"I came here before all the messy stuff with my parents went down. I always thought talking about this place would remind me of it." What happened with my family was part of it. Even if my family was fractured for a time, I would have returned, except for everything else that happened.

Libby looks at me. *So, we're just not going to talk about the ex-boyfriend next door?*

Nope.

"I'm sorry. I didn't realize." Amber says, looking guilty as her words trail off.

"It's fine," I reassure her and the rest of the group. It's the truth. It's not simple by any means, but I'm surviving. After talking to Diane this morning and walking around town, my body is at ease. I don't feel like I'm bracing for disaster. "Honestly, despite my weird history with this place, I'm happy we ended up here together. I would have wanted to bring you guys here if I'd known everyone back then."

In high school, I always considered the beach and the Pink House my secret places. I could have invited Cammie to come plenty of times, but I was scared to overlap my worlds.

I wanted it to be mine. Seeing my friends so happy here makes me regret not sharing the magic of this place sooner.

Our last stop is Books. The disorganized chaos of the tall shelves makes it easy to lose yourself. It's also terrible when you're trying to keep track of five other people.

We end up playing an impromptu game of hide and seek after we lose sight of each other. Sure, we could shout or attempt echolocation, but bookstores feel a little like libraries when it comes to loud sounds. If feels illegal to talk above a certain volume.

I find Jess in the romance section. She's carrying none other than Whispering Cove. It could be my old copy, unless everyone in this town had a shared experience with that book.

The two of us weave through the stacks until we have collected Libby from the tiny astrology and spirituality section, Caleb from a collection of Westerns, and Josh from the staff's picks. The only one left is Amber. After another fifteen minutes, we are about ready to give up. We try to call her phone. But, of course, the thick walls of the old building disrupt our phone signals.

"We could split up," Caleb suggests. I can tell he wants to make this a competition.

"Then we'd have to do this all over again." I sigh. We turn the corner to the science nonfiction section, and there she is, sitting on the floor with the shop cat in her lap and a used book on Australia's coral reefs in the other.

"Of course, you're in the farthest, most boring possible corner." Josh stands over her.

"I was never worried for a second you wouldn't find me," she croons back up at him. Amber gently dislodges the cat and unfolds herself from the floor. "Emma, did you ever work here?"

"No, why?"

"Because the sections are all in your handwriting," Amber says, pointing to 'Non-fiction Nature.' Admittedly, I never made it through most of the non-fiction, so some of those still have the old labels. She knows what it looks like from our class together, but mostly because she's observant as hell.

"That was just a little project of mine. I couldn't read them, so I replaced them."

"Oh, that must be why the historical fiction section is just marked classics." Libby nods like it all makes sense now.

"I had to guess on some of them." I shrug. Maybe it helped some people discover something new.

"You really left your mark on this place," Libby says, taking my hand as we make our way to the register.

"I guess I did."

We swing our arms back and forth like little kids. I feel lighter than I have in days.

True to form, Josh carries most of the bags as we walk back to the house. We're all wearing matching neon tourist hats with a gift shop logo.

"There's no way that any donuts are good enough to have to wait in this line," Caleb complains. We've already been waiting thirty minutes in line. The shop won't open for its evening hours for another twenty minutes, and the line already is circling the block.

"Dawn's is worth it. This will ruin all other donuts for you," I say. It's true I haven't found any to rival the one's here. Dawn's has mastered the balance of a cake donut that isn't dry or sickly sweet. To make them more addicting, they have constantly rotating flavors. My favorite was red velvet with a cinnamon cream cheese frosting, but they only made them for a week.

Caleb still seems unimpressed, "If you're wrong, you have to drive the first shift on the way back to Haven." I shake his hand, sealing the deal.

"Hey." Jordan is waving at us and jogging over. "Thanks for the heads up about the donut run," he says to Jess. Theo and Bennett appear next to him.

"God, what's with the hats? They're so bright they could stop traffic." Theo shields his eyes from the visually offensive neon.

"You haven't really visited a place if you don't embrace the tourist lifestyle a little. You guys are missing out," I tell them.

"Bennett, can we please get matching shirts?" Theo pleads as he and Jordan clasp their hands, looking like begging children.

"Only if they are just as obnoxious and embarrassing as those glow in the dark hats." He grins, flicking the brim of my hat.

A sprinkle of rain starts as we make it to the sidewalk in front of Dawn's, not quite to the striped awning. We're at the point of no return. What's a little rain?

The little rain quickly turns into the start of a brutal storm.

"Libby, I thought you check the weather app religiously," Amber shouts.

"I'm on strike. I can't take the responsibility of being the only person who knows the weather anymore. Too much pressure," she shrugs.

"Shit. Did none of us check the weather?" Josh asks. We've just reached the awning by the time the downpour becomes violent.

"We can't carry back our treasure in this," Theo realizes. He's right. The boxes would get soaked through in a minute. The alternative is eating them at the shop, but that feels too rushed to properly enjoy our winnings. And yes, they are winnings. We've had to fight off at least five other groups trying to sneak in front of us in line.

"What if we head back for the van, and someone stays to get the donuts?" Amber is already looking into the storm and planning the escape.

"I'll stay." I volunteer.

"I'll stay too. Just in case you have to fight off any more PTA moms," Bennett says, disregarding what I said yesterday. If I tell him to go with the group, I'll look like an asshole. And PTA moms aren't for the faint of heart.

Libby looks at me. *Is this ok?*

I nod. *I'll survive*

"Great, you locals will both know what's best," Amber says. I don't really count as a local, but I have tried my share of flavors.

The group sprints out into the rain. It only takes seconds for their forms to get lost in the deluge. Yet again, it's just Bennett and me. It doesn't matter that we are in a crowd of people ravenous for donuts. It feels like we're the only people on the planet.

When it's finally our turn, I beam up at the guy behind the counter, "Two dozen of whatever you have." He loads up two boxes with everything ranging from glazed to maple bacon drizzled with real syrup. There's no point in being picky. Everything is good, even the basics.

"I've got it." Bennett pulls out his card to pay.

"No. Here." I move faster, inserting my card into the reader. It's our version of a Western quick draw, and I unquestionably win.

"You didn't have to do that."

"I really did. There are six of us and only three of you. It makes perfect sense." We make our way outside. The view beyond the parking lot is still hidden by the storm.

"I was just trying to be nice."

"Stop trying so hard. There's no one else but me to show off to right now."

"I wasn't trying to show off."

"Then why try? Why do you insist on inserting yourself into everything we do? If you hate me so much, why don't you just leave me alone? What point are you trying to make?" I finally snap. He made the decision to continue to be around me, even after I had told him that I was content with not knowing each other.

"I don't hate you. I want to hate you, but I don't think I'm wired to do anything but want you. I hate myself for wanting you so badly when you want nothing to do with me. I hate that I can't leave our summers behind and move on like you have. You moved on." As he speaks, I stiffen. That's not what I had wanted. I want us to both be free of this.

"It's not fair."

"No, what's not fair is you didn't let me say it the first time I tried to. You got to run off to reality, not answering any of my calls or texts while I was stuck watching new families go in and out of your house every time I was home. Every time I looked, it was just another reminder you weren't there." His words come as a punch to my gut. I hadn't given a second thought to the fact that he couldn't just throw the remnants of us into a box and leave it in some forgotten corner to collect dust.

For me, our memories are things that creep in when my mind goes silent. So, I've chosen to live a loud life. For him, they must be a raw wound. Each time he returns, the scar is ripped open, never given a chance to fully heal.

"What do you want me to do? Burn it down to put you out of your misery?"

"That would be nice."

"I want a truce," I demand.

"A truce?"

"I just want these last few days with them. You can hate whatever you want, but don't bring them into it. I'm lucky they brought me after I blew them off the last few years. We said we could be normal that first night. Can't we just try again? I can tell they really like you guys, and I don't want to take that away." What I don't say is that is an act of self-preservation. I'm not sure how much more of him I can survive.

"I'll see what I can manage."

"Promise?" I ask a touch of desperation in my voice.

He nods. I nearly hold up my hand to complete our ritual, but he's holding the boxes of donuts. More importantly, we're not those people anymore.

We sit in silence, our words hanging in the air. We don't exchange as much as a look until the van pulls up in the parking lot.

Despite being soaking wet, everyone is in great spirits at the promise of biting into god tier confection. As we join everyone in the van, Bennett shifts into the magnetic version of himself. Anytime he laughs at someone's joke or flashes a genuine smile, he draws people in. They see what I saw years ago; he cares and isn't afraid of showing it.

That pull is why it's so hard for me to look away. He's temptation with rain darkened hair and a sideways smile.

This just might work, but God will it tear me to pieces.

8
Summer
Six years ago

I've always wondered what it would be like to have older brothers or even siblings around my age. Corrina is seven years older than me. No parts of our lives ever overlapped in a meaningful way. While I was starting high school, she was already getting ready to pack up and leave for college. The distance in time now feels impossible to rectify even though we're older and have a chance.

The Sorenson boys have started to be like brothers to me. It's in the moments where we bicker and have meaningless fights over pizza toppings or what movie to watch. But the illusion shatters when I leave at the end of the day. It's only a vicarious relationship, a window into the strong bonds some siblings share.

Tanner is just about to start college this fall. His friends are off on senior trips while he's stuck in town. He started joining in on our adventures. I hadn't realized how much Tanner needed to be around people. He asks to join even when I sit at Early Bird just to read. We sit in silence until Bennett is done for the day. It is one of those nearly indiscernible differences between the younger Sorenson brothers. Where Bennett is a magnetic force that draws people in, Tanner craves to be part of a group.

He also brings more than a bit of mischief and shit talking with him, which is why Bennett and I are packing buckets of sand onto him. As anyone experienced in sand burials knows, you have to dig a hole for your victim to lay in first. You can't just start by piling on the sand.

"I swear I wasn't cheating! Counting cards is skills based," Tanner calls out. He's nothing more than a head sticking out of the sand now. We had been playing Uno. Tanner's first win turned into six before we figured it out. Who even knows how many cards are in an Uno deck? So, yes, he deserves to be buried to his neck in sand.

"How long should we leave him like this?" I ask my partner in revenge. If Tanner wasn't ok with his fate, he could have gotten away at any point before now.

Bennett takes a second to think, "I say we check back in ten minutes and see if he's learned his lesson. If not, we can come back and build a castle on top." We start walking away. Suddenly, I'm in the air, and the world is upside down. Tanner has broken free of his prison and flung me over his shoulder. I shriek before I'm set down moments later.

"I guess the punishment didn't stick," I'm laughing to the point of hiccups. I turn to look at Bennett, but instead of playing along the way I'm used to, he's glaring at his brother.

"If you want to try again, be my guest. But it's going to cost you," Tanner says right before he starts to chase me back to the Pink House. We're laughing, and out of breath by the time Bennett makes his way up the steps. He'd usually be right here with us. It must be an off day.

After the last couple of summers, I've gotten used to the water. I have decided it's time to learn how to surf. I walk over to the Sorenson house on a mission. Before I came to the beach house, I hadn't gone into the ocean or learned how to ride a bike. Now, they are part of my everyday routine. How bad could this be?

When I knock, a voice calls for me to come in. I find Tanner in the kitchen with a half-eaten waffle sticking out of his mouth.

"Is Bennett here?" I ask.

He shakes his head.

"I'll just come back later." I begin to turn back to the door.

"What's up? I want in on whatever you're planning, I'm bored as hell. You don't have to wait until Bennett's done with work."

"I was going to ask if he could teach me how to surf."

"I can teach you. I've been doing it longer, so I'll probably be the better teacher." He takes the last bite of his waffle. "Let me grab some stuff, and I'll meet you outside. Also, maybe make sure you don't wear one of those tiny swimsuits. It'll come right off the first time you wipe out."

My cheeks heat thinking about someone looking at me in a bikini. My swimsuits are all definitely normal sized. Plenty of girls my age on the beach wear things far smaller.

"How do you know I'll wipe out?"

"Emma. Everyone wipes out. It's a rite of passage." He rolls his eyes

An hour later, I still haven't made it on the water. I'm learning how to pop up and not tip over. Apparently, I'm not going to master surfing in one day.

Tanner is a good teacher. I expected him to make fun of me each time I nearly fell or clumsily got to my feet. Instead, he's attentive and gives me advice, patient even when I'm slow to pick up on things.

"Think of it as one smooth movement, not separate steps. Let me show you again." He gets down, and he's on his feet in one fluid move. I would never have called Tanner graceful before that moment, but that's what he is right now. I can feel myself staring for too long. "Your turn."

"If I get it this time, can we finally get in the water?" I beg. Even if I don't make this one, I need to jump in to cool off. We started early, but the sun has become merciless after being out for hours.

I get down and start to move. This is the one. I feel my mind and body click into harmony. I'm going to land it. I'm really going to do it.

"Hey, guys!" Bennett calls out, breaking my focus. Just seconds before, I was in perfect alignment, but now my foot lands awkwardly. I start to fall. Strong arms catch me. Of course, Bennett would catch me. He's always there when I need him.

But when I look up, Bennett is still a few feet away. I turn to see Tanner is the one holding me up.

"You can let her go now," Bennett says in a low voice. Tanner lets me down, being careful about my twisted ankle.

"Yeah, I'm good. Thank you," I say.

There is a crackle of uncomfortable tension in the air.

The energy between the three of us is off the rest of the day. When I can't handle it any longer, I go home. I can only count a few times over the last few years that I've come home this early when I have the option to do otherwise.

With nothing else to do, I call Cammie.

She had been at a silent creators retreat for the first week of summer that didn't allow phones. I give her a crash course of summer so far in Harriettesville while she tells me all about the guy at the retreat who snored all night. No one could sleep, but there was no way to tell him without breaking their vow of silence.

"Damn, Em. You have two brothers all over you."

"It's not like that. And even if I like one of them, they're my only friends at the beach. It would mess everything up." I had told her about my budding feelings for Bennett, but Tanner has never even been a passing thought.

"Whatever you say. You don't talk about anyone at school like you do with your summer boys. If you want one of them, you better make a move before someone else snatches them up. I've seen the pictures. I might not be attracted to men, but I know a hot person when I see one." She's right. I've never had the same confused mess of emotions about anyone else. "Just keep me updated. I'm living vicariously through you. I swear all of the hot girls here have run away to New York and Spain."

"Aren't you in Montana?" Her parents have formed a new obsession with the Northern Lights.

"Don't remind me," she grumbles.

The thought of Cammie having to live vicariously through me is laughable. I love my summers at the beach, they are everything to me, but they aren't the same as the immersive and crazy trips she goes on. I will admit I don't envy her trip this year.

I eat a popsicle out on the porch while waiting for Bennett. It's the kind with real fruit that when you bite into a piece, your teeth hurt from the cold. Books is having its annual sale today, and we were determined to make it this year after missing it the last two summers.

Tanner sits down next to me. He moves like a shark and bites off the top of the popsicle.

"Watch it. I was eating that." I hold it above my head, out of reach.

"You were eating it too slow." His lips draw up into a sideways smile, "I'm just helping out. What's on the agenda for the day?"

"We're going to Books."

"Cool, mind if I join?"

"This is kind of something Bennett and I have been planning for a while, and I should probably ask him first." I don't feel guilty, but it's weird telling him this. I like including him, but this plan is different. It's one of those things that feel like it's supposed to be only for me and Bennett.

"I get it." I move to say something, but he cuts me off. "No, really, it's fine."

It's another few minutes before Bennett pops his head out to let me know he'll be ready after he changes. He only has to do this when there are a particularly large number of spills at work.

As Bennett and I sort through the sale books, I notice Tanner's absence. Not because I miss him but because there is a lack of heaviness. Ever since that first surf lesson, there has been an odd tension between the brothers, like they fought about something.

When we return to the house, I follow Bennett upstairs to drop off his books. I've never gone up to Bennett's room before. I never had a reason to.

I had made up versions of it. My favorite version was the one splattered with band posters and had a skateboard leaning in the corner, despite Bennett never mentioning a skateboard. His room is at the back of the house, giving him a view of the beach through the window. My imagination wasn't too far off with the rest of the design. There are a few band posters and vintage surf magazine covers. But most of the decorations are pictures.

My gaze easily finds the pictures I mailed him last year when I had the film from my disposable camera developed. Most are blurry snapshots of us mixed in with Polaroids; some are on flimsy printer paper. A few are in frames: Tanner's high school graduation, a family camping trip, and one more that makes my breath hitch. It's the lone picture he took of me surrounded by his dad's vinyl.

When I first saw it, I thought I looked gross, with the start of a laugh scrunching up my face and my slumped posture. Now I want to like it more. I don't want to assume he thinks it's something precious, but the care he took to frame it allows me to believe he does.

Bennett's voice breaks the spell, "I have something I've been meaning to give you. I was going to ship it to you on your birthday, but I really wanted to give it to you in person."

I continue to take everything in as he rummages through his drawers. As I wait, I sit on his bed, sinking into the mattress topped with a plaid comforter.

"Here it is." He pulls out a small jewelry box. I open it and see a necklace nestled in a bed of tissue paper. It's the piece of sea glass that we found. He's wrapped it in wire and secured it to a chain.

"This is perfect." I hold it to the light so the pale blue glass catches a soft glow.

"May I?" He gestures to the necklace. The words sound so formal coming from him. I hand it back to him and sweep up my curls so they don't get caught. The comforter shifts beneath me as I move to the side so he can clasp his gift around my neck. A shock runs through me as his fingers graze the back of my neck.

When I get home, I can't help but stare at myself in the necklace. I wear it every day, only taking it off before showering or going into the ocean.

It's the last night on the beach, and we have some leftover fireworks from the Fourth. Having fireworks whenever we want is just another magical thing about the beach. I'm finally feeling more comfortable around the explosives. It's only taken three years.

As we light the last fuse, Tanner pulls out a joint. He lights it and takes a hit. Smoke falls from his lips, coiling up into the sky, mixing with the fumes from the fireworks. The mix of smells makes my nose twitch.

"I'm good," Bennett says when Tanner offers it to him.

Tanner then gestures to me, "Emma?"

I took a hit at a party back home, ending in an embarrassingly long coughing fit. But why the hell not? This is the place where I've always learned how to do things.

"Sure," I say. I see a flash of surprise on Bennett's face. I inhale. It seems ok, so I get bolder and take another hit. A cough rattles out of me.

"Here," Tanner offers me his water.

"I'm so bad at that."

"It's how everyone is the first time. They just don't like to admit it," Tanner says. This is one of those moments when I see him choose to be kind. To hold my hand through something he could otherwise taunt me for.

I feel my head grow lighter. The breeze is soft against my skin. I want to sink into the sand and be cocooned in it. I run my hand up and down the worn towel. It's rough but comforting. I start swaying with the sound of the ocean. Time is blurry and soft.

"I'm going to head to bed. Have to drive Justin to the airport in the morning. Don't do anything stupid." Bennett's words disrupt my bubble of bliss. That last part doesn't seem directed at me. I know that even through my haze.

When he gets up, there is a space between Tanner. I don't like it, so I close the gap. I can feel the heat of his body. I lean into the warmth until my shoulder brushes his. He turns to me at some point. I look up, getting lost in tracing the planes of his face.

"Can I kiss you?" Tanner's eyes are dancing hopefully and looking into mine for confirmation.

"What?" My mind goes blank.

"I just thought..." He trails off.

"No. I'm sorry." I shift away from him.

"It's him, isn't it?" We both know which him he's talking about.

"I should go." I get to my feet and need a moment to reorient myself before going home.

It's the last night of summer, and the wrong Sorenson boy just asked to kiss me.

I know with sharp clarity it would be wrong if it wasn't Bennett. It had always been Bennett for me, and it took me until now to fit it into place. I want to go to his room and wake him up. Tell him about Tanner and how all I want is him.

I need to tell Bennett.

The last time I kept something like this from him, we had our first fight. But nothing happened between Tanner and me. Would it be worse to say something? My head is still buzzing from the weed.

"Cammie, I need your help." I think I'm crying when she picks up.

"Hey, hey, what happened? Are you ok?" Her voice is scratchy from sleep. I know I'm crying now, the tears falling onto my legs. I tell her about Tanner and Bennett. I tell her I'm high. I tell her that she's been right the entire time.

"Just get some sleep. You can tell him in the morning. Sleep, and you'll figure out what to say. Being high is only adding to the paranoia."

"Ok." I had found my way back to my room. I don't change before falling into bed. I don't remember hanging up or setting an alarm. I know I must have set an alarm because it wakes me up the next morning.

I throw myself out of bed and don't bother changing. I race to catch Bennett before he leaves.

He's gone.

I'm back to where I started when I fell asleep.

Nothing happened between Tanner and me. If I tell Bennett, things will change. But will it be worse if I don't say anything? Something I've never admitted to anyone, not even Cammie, is that wanting Bennett means risking losing him. Not just him, all of the Sorensons. It means I might lose all future summers. It's a cost I'm not willing to pay.

9
Wednesday
Now

We're back at the beach when my phone rings.

Again.

For the eighth time this morning.

I've been dodging calls from my mom, sending her excuses about cell reception and being in the middle of nonexistent plans. It's come to the point where I either need to block her or pick up. Though blocking her for the rest of the week is tempting, I'm not sure I'll be able to handle the fallout.

I groan as I accept the call.

"Your father is wondering what Jackson's parents are planning for graduation so we can coordinate."

"Mom," I try to interrupt, but she is a professional bulldozer when she wants to be heard.

"It's rude to not consider what they have planned. Really, Emma Claire, you've been so selfish lately." I can tell this was about to get much worse with what I am about to say.

"Mom, we broke up."

"Why on earth would you do that? What did you do?" Predictably, I had to be the one to do something wrong.

"I did nothing but walk in on him with someone else."

"Did you talk it over with him?" Why would I expect her to ask if I was ok? Maybe because she liked our relationship, I thought she might care. Nope, she just cares about keeping that relationship together. When I was with Jackson, I was fulfilling her idea of a picture perfect family.

"You can't be serious."

"These things happen sometimes. Your father and I have had our differences, but we're fine now." That's one way to put it.

"Sorry if I don't take your advice. You and Dad aren't exactly Couple of The Year." If I wanted to end up like my parents, I would have taken them up on the series of blind dates they tried to set me up on freshman year. Hell, I started turning into them the moment I stayed with Jackson out of convenience.

"Emma Claire, watch your tone. You have no idea how this will change your plans. Does this mean you're not in Tennessee?" I want to scream at her. They aren't my plans. My parents had handed me an itinerary for my future and expected me to play along.

"No, I'm in Harriettesville," I pause. "With Bennett." I hang up. She knows everything that I'm implying. I'll let her believe it, even if it couldn't be farther from the truth.

Maybe I should have blocked her. Her calls and texts triple throughout the day. I shut off my phone. There's no use in having it on. The only people I want to talk to right now are lying on an island of faded beach towels a few feet away.

True to form, my friends are still on a mission to make life as eventful as possible. They have discovered the local dive bar hosts karaoke nights every Wednesday.

I haven't seen any sign that Bennett and his friends will be joining us for the night. It feels like a betrayal to go without him. This isn't the first time I have felt this way. Over the years, there have been so many things that have felt wrong to do without him.

We had one of those unwritten lists of things we would do together. We would throw out ideas, not writing them down, but both of us remembered them with startling clarity whenever one came up. I can still recall the highlights. Going to college and eventually moving in together, karaoke, going to every national park on the east coast. I remember crying on my 21st birthday last year after drinking the night away because he wasn't there to take that first legal drink with me. Libby and Jess had to carry me to bed that night as I cried.

I had always kept the memories of us so close to my heart. The sting is worse today, knowing I could walk over to his house, knock on his door, and invite him to join.

The pain deepens as I realize that he has likely gone there already. Of course, he has. He's come back here every holiday and break. What's the point of avoiding one of the few bars in town just because of a half formed promise we made years ago? I bet he and Tanner went the summer after his 21st birthday. They probably did a terrible rendition of "Sweet Caroline" that had everyone singing along with them.

Looking at my friends, I'm reminded that this isn't home to any of us, at least not anymore.

I've been in town when the summer tourists flowed in. People watching and guessing where people were from was a lazy day activity, for when the sun was too heavy to do much besides be in the water or the shade. They had always dressed up as if trying to make some point, but it only made them stand out more. I think I liked the game so much because I was also trying to point out how much I belonged.

It's spring break.

Who cares if anyone goes all out? Who am I trying to fool? I was never a local. There's no reason to continue pretending.

Libby is in the tamest of the going out tops she had packed, a simple black band of fabric. She claims the only color she needs to make a statement is in her hair. The flames she had at the beginning of the trip have faded into a less defined reddish orange ombre from getting in the water and showering off sand and sunblock.

Amber and Jess love glitter and bold colors, and vacationing in a laidback beach town has not impacted their taste. I never wanted them to change. I want them to stand out because they deserve to be seen and appreciated.

Amber is in a pink sequin top that makes her new tan pop. When Josh sees her, he makes a cartoon honking sound and tries to take her back upstairs.

Jess's yellow, silky bandeau perfectly complements her dark skin. God, my friends are fucking smoke shows.

Another thing that drunk me had neglected was anything bar worthy. The girls all offer whatever extras they brought, and I pick out Amber's pale blue halter that makes me feel a particular blend of hot and confident whenever I borrow it.

On the walk over, the air hints at the rain forecast for later tonight. We took a shot or two before leaving the house. The light buzz makes me feel lighter and more optimistic about the night's outcome.

The Deck is all faded wood and vintage signs. You're guaranteed to walk out smelling a bit like cigarette smoke. The Deck isn't some college bar masquerading as a dive. It's the real deal.

There's a pool table in the middle of the room and a small, raised stage at the far end. Calling it a stage is generous. It's more of a platform where live music acts play. Tonight, the act is any drunk person attempting to carry a tune. The space is packed with people our age, likely also on spring break, with no other plans for the night.

Libby puts our name in the queue as two girls scream a Carrie Underwood song. On the walk over, we determined that the girls, minus Amber, who has the most severe case of stage fright I've ever seen, will go up together. This is the only way to get the guys to perform their own musical numbers. I'm still convinced they'll buy us enough drinks to make us forget their half of the deal.

"I'm grabbing a drink. Anyone want anything?" They rattle off drink orders, and I head to the bar. It's easy to pick out a familiar face in a crowd of strangers. So, it's hard to look away when one of the local boys locks eyes with me. Davis had been somewhat scrawny as a teenager, but the last few years had done him a favor. He had been all shy smiles and messy dark hair. Now a perpetual grin was splashed across his face. He's broad and has a shadow of stubble that makes him look older than twenty-three.

"What the hell? Emma Danes, is that really you, or have I had too many drinks and am starting to daydream?"

"Davis. How are you?"

"What are the odds? In all of the bars in town." His lips rise in a smirk.

"I know, right? You still live in town?"

"Yeah, helping my dad with his contracting business." I had forgotten that his dad was one of the few contractors in town. His family does well with it, from what I remember. Before I can ask more, the bartender sets down the last tequila sour. I can only hope he's traveled to all those museums like he had talked about.

"I've got to get these drinks to my friends. I'll see you, ok?"

"Sure thing." He gives me a smile and turns to the group he's come with.

A few drinks later, it's our turn to go up. I trusted them to pick the song, knowing there's a limited selection and nothing past 2010. I hear the first notes and look at the screen to see the lyrics to Carly Simon's "You're So Vain" scrawl across the purple background.

During the first chorus, reality shifts. Everything fades as a group walks through the door. I've only seen the new Bennett in swim trunks or thrown on lazy post-beach clothes. The tight, dark t-shirt and shorts he is wearing now do things to me that I don't want to admit.

We lock eyes.

He's taking me in, raking his eyes over my body like I did to him.

In my periphery, Libby and Jess are singing with the resentment of a scorned lover that the song deserves, while I can only manage mournful longing through the tangled feeling in my throat.

I'm singing to him.

Singing to the memory of us. Singing to the people we never became, the ones we swore to become. It's as if a spotlight is shining on him, and I can't break away. For a few moments, we are the only people in the bar.

Jess breaks the spell as she sways her hips into mine, encouraging me to dance to the music. As the song ends, we return to our booth.

"I forgot to say something earlier, but the guys told me they were running behind." When did Jess even get one of their numbers? Whose number did she get? It must be the alcohol that makes over think this comment. It's also probably what's making me feel excited when I should be bracing for another sparring match with Bennett.

"I thought we were 'the guys,'" Caleb mopes. It's no secret that he's had the biggest crush on Jess.

"It's totally different. They're hot spring break guys; you're just our guys." Jess says, but I'm not sure it has the comforting effect she intends.

I take a sip of my drink, and the heavy pour of liquor burns through my chest, exactly what I need to make it through the night.

Davis finds his way back to me. Everyone else has dispersed to mingle with the other spring breakers. Libby is in a corner flirting with a girl with bubblegum pink braids, backlit by a collection of neon signs. Amber and Josh are dancing. Jess is chatting with Bennett. I have to keep reminding myself that it's ok if they do end up together, but my eyes keep flicking back to them.

"That was definitely something out of an early 2000s romcom," he says.

"You watch romcoms? Not saying that's weird, just unexpected."

"I have three older sisters, remember? I was outvoted so many times I stopped fighting it. Also, gotta give the writing some credit. They're funny." He playfully nudges me with his shoulder. I know he has sisters, or at least I knew that at some point. I'm embarrassed that I've forgotten. "I still can't believe you're back here. And damn, Emma, you look great. Like you've always looked good but now. I have to admit, seeing you tied to Sorenson always had me a bit jealous," he lets the words tumble out.

"Thanks. You seem so much more confident. It suits you," I brush off the not so hidden message underlying his words. I don't notice that the gap between us has grown smaller until I look up to see his glittering hazel eyes inches from mine.

I stand straighter, feeling the space behind me shift. Davis turns his attention to look over my shoulder.

"Hey. It's been a minute." Bennett's voice doesn't hold the lightness it should have when greeting an old friend. Jess is now flirting with the bartender, Watson. Who I recognize from those distant summer bonfires.

"It's cool seeing everyone back in town," Davis says.

"Feels like nothing has changed." Bennett takes a step closer, so he is almost pressed against me. What possessive bullshit is this? He told me he didn't want me here. We have our truce. Despite these things, my mind wanders, thinking about what it would be like to lean back and feel his body against me.

"Yeah, good to see you here, man. Good talking to you, Emma." Davis can't escape fast enough. Bennett sent the message loud and clear. *Off limit*s. Even if I'm not his anymore, no one else can have me.

"Why did you do that?" I whirl on Bennett as he takes a sip of his drink. His ring adorned hand is clutching a sweating cup of dark liquid. I'm glad I'm not the only one needing hard liquor to get through the night.

"Do what?" He gives me a cocky smirk.

I'm not in the mood for this game. He's always been good at playing around, but this is different. We both know what my conversation with Davis was leading to. I just wouldn't be the one to admit it. The other night had revealed he still wanted me. But he had said it like it was the worst fate in the world. Like I'm some virus that he can't get rid of.

"I was just catching up with an old friend before you showed up."

"That looked like it was about to turn into more than 'catching up.'"

"What if it was? I'm an adult and allowed to choose who I get to *more than catch up* with." That wasn't my intention with Davis, but what if it was? The girls are right. I need a rebound. Hooking up with Davis would have been uncomplicated. He is exactly what they have been begging me to find.

"I don't blame him. I can't stay away from you when you look like this, either." There's his devilish side again, making my blood run hot. Taunting me, playing me so perfectly. I want him to mean his words.

"I thought we had a truce."

"You said to act normal around your friends. They all seem a little preoccupied."

He's so close. I take in that musky, smoky scent. His fingers brush the exposed skin on my lower back so lightly that if I hadn't seen him move to do it, I would have denied it happening at all. I lurch, bumping into the table. I hit it hard enough with my hip that I know there will be a bruise in the morning.

That's what I need, another bruise. After my pre-spring break bar crawl and the volleyball incident, it's not like I've collected enough of them.

"I only came because Jess asked." He attempts to correct course, directing us out of dangerous waters, "That came out wrong. I mean, I don't come to karaoke nights here. Actually, I've never gone to one anywhere. I only came because I knew you'd be here." Some of the tightness in my chest loosens. Despite the years apart, the memories still connect us. I feel less alone knowing that we both clung to that idea of who we planned to be.

"If you had to go up there and sing something right now, what would it be?" I don't mean to ask the question out loud. I'm inviting the memory of us back in.

"You remember that summer you insisted on teaching me about jukebox musicals? How we played them so much that Tanner threatened to punch the TV to make it stop? I'd sing "Roxanne," but only if you went up there with me." We had gone through *Moulin Rouge, Mama Mia,* and *Across the Universe*. Tanner had threatened to break the speakers in addition to the TV when we played the soundtracks on repeat.

"Is that a promise?" I am feeling brave from the drinks but also desperate to grab hold of this thread of hope he is offering.

"Would I ever lie to you?" Yes, Bennett Sorenson, you would. But right now, I will believe anything he says. His nostalgia laced words make me putty in his hands.

"We have a truce. Remember?" He echoes my words back to me. "Singing karaoke is something normal people who don't hate each other do." I attempt to move out of his way just as he reaches out to squeeze my hand. "Please." Something soft and unreadable crosses his features.

"Ok." I give in. He looks so much like he used to when we were us.

Instead of letting my hand go after I agree, he stands up and guides me to the stage.

We are really doing this.

Finally.

He tells the guy operating the equipment what we'll be singing.

We step up on the platform.

For a few minutes, I'm sixteen, back before we kissed and fell so hopelessly for each other. We're just friends dancing around his living room, belting out lyrics. I don't have to think about next week or what will happen after graduation. I'm sixteen, and I know I'll be here back here next summer with the boy who has become my whole world.

Inevitably, the song ends, allowing time to collapse in on itself. The past and present collide with force. I don't know if my heavy breathing is from the all-out performance we put on or the weight of the air hanging between us. I look up and see his eyes echoing my own need.

I break away and leave. He can always rely on me to do that. I'm a fool for pretending, and if I lingered for a moment longer, I don't know if I'd be able to stay away from him.

Mercifully, he leaves me alone for the rest of the night.

"I simply can't compete. He's all yours," Jess says. We were at the back of the group walking home. It's past midnight, and there's a light mist of rain. Between the blur of drinks and having a good time with Bennett, I feel like I'm dreaming.

"What do you mean?" I look at her, not entirely sure what she's talking about.

"I mean that you two are desperately in love with each other. I never stood a chance." She's pouty but not actually upset. We had made a pact years ago that we would never fight over a guy after we discovered some frat bro had been texting us both, even though he knew we were roommates at the time. Jess sent him a picture of us and a text that reminded him, 'If you're going to be a pig, at least be smart about it.'

"We're just friends. We knew each other before we were together. That's long done."

"If my *just friends* looked at me like that, I would have slept with every single one of them," she giggles. "Either way, I need to find a new target."

I want to mention Caleb, but I don't want to mess with his business. There could be a reason he's playing the long game. Or maybe he is caught up in the reality that they are about to end up on opposite corners of the country. He could just be waiting out the pining until he can put distance between them. I understand the feeling.

That night I dream of soft lips and the caress of ring clad hands against my cheeks. I burst from the dream just as those hands creep dangerously lower.

I can't go back to sleep. I hear the buzz of the television downstairs, so I get up to investigate. As expected, Libby is wide awake. I settle in next to her, leaning my head on her shoulder.

"How are you doing?" She asks as the episode of whatever she's been watching ends.

"I'm not sure." I'm not fine. I needed someone to hear me when I admitted it.

How many times can your heart break for one person?

Tonight, he'd dug up our memories with his bare hands. I let him remind me why it was so hard to let go. In that moment, I fell for him all over again. Now, I'm more lost than ever.

10

Summer

Five years ago

It's the last summer before senior year. I plan on applying to Portland College in Maine, where Bennett is about to start his first year. He called me the second he'd gotten his acceptance for their environmental policy program. It's one of the country's only programs focusing on marine conservation.

I'm not someone that would follow their friends to college, or that's what I tell myself. It feels like fate. I've wanted to go there for as long as I can remember. When Corrina was applying to colleges, I had seen a Portland College brochure she'd been sent on the counter and borrowed it. Well, I never gave it back. I fell in love with the pictures of campus and the descriptions of the city. It's pinned up above my desk, a reminder of what is just around the corner.

When Bennett said he got accepted, I saw the next chapter of our future. I'll apply to other places, too, mostly to appease my parents. Seeing his dreams come to life and hearing his passion is amazing.

Still, it also makes me start confronting a reality I've been avoiding. I have no plan for what I want to do once I get there. When I talked to Cammie, she said it's normal not to know, but it's not comforting to hear that from someone who has known what they want to do since birth.

I've always known where I don't want to be. I don't want to have my life and work blend into an indistinguishable mess like my dad or always be in competition with others like Corrina. For the last few years, I've just been dreaming about the beach, and the fact that Portland checks that box is enough.

My first stop is Early Bird. We got in earlier than expected, and I want to surprise Bennett since he said he'll be working a long morning shift. When I walk in, my heart catches in my throat. A pretty redheaded girl is behind the bar with him, laughing at something he's said. He's funny, but I know that kind of laugh. She's shamelessly flirting with him.

I shouldn't be feeling these things. What do I care if someone is flirting with him, and he flirts back? But I do care. It's one more thing that adds to the tangle of emotions I've been burying. A mess that had gotten worse when I realized how much I do feel for him.

When Bennett turns away, I walk to the counter.

"Hi, what can I get you?" She flashes a smile with the most insane photo ready straight teeth. Damn. My self-esteem must have really taken a hit if I'm focusing on some girl's teeth.

"Hi," the word barely comes out, caught in my throat. "Can I get The Bennett?" I start to pull out my card as Bennett sprints over.

"Don't let her pay," he calls out, rushing over. "This is Emma. She gets her first drink of the summer for free always, Diane's orders. And she's also not allowed to insist on paying." It was starting to become something of tradition, if you could count four times a tradition. I love feeling like I have a special spot at the shop.

I also like to see if I can buy the first coffee of the summer without him noticing. So far, he's winning this game.

"I'm Nicole." She looks between Bennett and me before deciding what to say. "Are you Bennett's girlfriend?" The question is hopeful in a way I hate, and I don't want to tell the truth.

"No, just the neighbor," I say in what must be a too cheerful voice because Bennett winces. It is a terrible way to distill our friendship, but it's the truth.

He turns to me. "Give yourself more credit than that. Emma is practically part of the family," he says. I like the idea of being part of the Sorenson family, but the feeling that he might just see me as a little sister makes my stomach sink.

It makes sense that he sees me that way. He's literally taught me how to ride my bike and shoot off fireworks, things that give off big brother, little sister energy.

On the drive over, I had been reciting how to tell him everything I wanted to do last summer.

Hey, Bennett, I might be a little bit in love with you. If you don't feel the same way, can we forget this conversation happened? I can't lose you as a friend. Also, your brother tried to kiss me last year.

Now, the words vanish. Family. I can settle for being a part of the Sorenson family. For the last few years, that's all I've wanted.

Knowing that after this year, there is the possibility of seeing each other every day changes something. The days are lighter, with less pressure to squeeze the maximum joy out of each moment.

The carefree knowledge of our plans for next fall isn't the only thing that changes. My mother's mood is so much brighter. She's always flitting out of the house with a smile, headed to book clubs, spa days, or day trips to vineyards.

I never noticed what she was doing because I was only usually home to sleep and change. But now, she sends me text updates telling me when she'll be out of town for a few nights or if she plans to be out late. I've never seen her look so rejuvenated, so happy to be doing things. It's exciting to see her start to fall for the place I already love. It had taken time, but we were beginning to belong here.

I'm swinging my legs on my kitchen counter as Bennett takes stock of what I have in the fridge. He has a little sticky note list and writes down whatever he thinks I need.

"Emma, you live off of this stuff?"

"I live off of your mom's baking and dad's cooking." For breakfast, I usually have something from Early Bird and then have dinner or lunch at the Sorensons. The time at my own house just fills the gaps. We never have anything elaborate here. I'm a mediocre cook on a good day.

"We're going to have a pasta making crash course one day. You need to learn how to cook."

"I make a mean sandwich. And when we're at Portland together, you can do all the cooking so I don't starve."

"That's not cooking, and I'm not going to be your private chef." He turns back to his list and scribbles. "You're out of bread." Bennett's list is currently three sticky notes long, and it's a good thing that he's inherited Tanner's old car because there is no way we will be able to walk back with all the bags. With my mother gone, I'm on grocery duty.

Bennett's phone starts to ring. He never silences it, especially now that Tanner is getting his boating license.

"I'll be right back," he says, walking into the living room. He paces whenever he's on the phone doing laps with animated gestures as if the person on the other end can see. He comes back with an odd expression.

"Is everything ok?" I ask.

"Yeah, but my mom just called, and I have to get to the café. I don't want to ditch you last minute, but the closer just called with the flu, and Mom's a couple of towns over picking up a supply order. I'd ask Tanner, but there's no way he's not high off his ass or on the water somewhere."

The plan was to get groceries, make sandwiches, and picnic on the beach. I love that he's apologetic over missing something we can do anytime, like everything we do matters.

"No, go, it's totally fine. I'll even come with you and help. Then you can get out of there faster. We can go shopping later."

"You're sure?"

"Yes, but only on one condition," I nod.

"You have conditions?"

"As I said, I only have one."

"Let's hear it then. I don't want to commit to anything too heinous."

"You teach me how to make your drink." I had tried to make the latte at home, but no matter what I did, it was just off. I had been tempted to text Bennett or Diane for help, but I had been determined not to be defeated by a drink. This wasn't cheating, just an alternative method.

"It's a deal." He sticks out his pinkie to shake, and once I take it, we leave.

It's fairly calm when we arrive, but the barista behind the counter looks frazzled.

"Get out of here, Ronny. We've got it covered." Bennett tosses me an extra baseball cap and pulls on his own. "Emma, can you snag the cash register? And if anyone asks, we're done with food for the day."

I step behind the counter and look at the register, which is a tablet looking device. I've never worked a register before. It seems simple enough.

It becomes abruptly clear I'm out of my depth when the first customer rattles off a string of words like 'cortado' and 'breve' that make no sense to me. I'm searching for the right buttons, and my eyes refuse to focus on the screen.

I must stare at the screen longer than needed because she clears her throat. "Is there a problem?"

"I'm sorry, it's my first day, and I'm still having trouble. I'll be right back." She looks back at me, thoroughly unimpressed. Great. This is just great.

I grab Bennett, "I'm sorry, but that lady just said things that didn't sound like English, and I have no idea what I'm doing. I know what a latte is, but what is a 'breve?' I really don't want to make this harder by being here," I say.

He laughs, "Well, that's probably because it was Italian. Let me help you with this one." Bennett joins me upfront and walks me through the process of putting through an order. It must have felt painfully slow to the woman, but I still struggle to take in the information.

"Sorry about the wait. It's on us today for your troubles." He flashes a winning smile, and the sour look on her face instantly dissolves.

After he resolves the situation, I watch him create drinks without a second thought while chatting with the regulars approaching him. He is more decisive here, every movement precise.

As I put in her order, a girl about my age leans in to get a better look at Bennett, "That barista is hot, isn't he? Do you know if he's single?"

"I guess he is. I'm not sure," I say, my thoughts drifting to Nicole. We don't really talk about relationships, so I wouldn't know. My gaze follows the girl's as we both stare at him.

The rest of the shift goes by far more smoothly. I count change at least three times before handing it to any customer. It feels like I've lost the ability to do simple math. There aren't many orders in the afternoon, and after the first hour, I'm confident behind the register.

"It's time to pay up." The door is locked, and Bennet is dusted with coffee grounds and little splashes of milk. The image reminds me of Diane with her inability to bake without being coated in a healthy layer of flour.

I follow him back behind the counter. He dispenses grounds into the espresso filter. "First, you have to use this to tamp the grounds." He holds up a metal piece that looks like a stamp. I push down like he said. "Come on, Danes, press a bit harder than that." He stands behind me, so I am sandwiched between the counter and him. His hand snakes over mine to help me add more force. My mind flashes to an image of him helping Nicole the same way. I force myself back to reality.

He's here in this moment with *me*.

We watch as the espresso shot drips from the machine, forming distinct layers. I'm in awe. I did that.

Bennett brings the espresso to his nose. "It's perfect."

He hands it to me. I take in the rich aroma, bold and silky. I'm not sure what I'm supposed to be searching for, but I still enjoy it.

I'm riding a high as he helps me measure the syrups and add a dash of cinnamon before combining the mixture with milk. I can't tell what part of the buzz is from the caffeine and what is pure Bennett.

As I scrub the remnants of coffee from mugs, he turns up the music, singing along to the lyrics, dancing with the broom, or moving his shoulders to the beat as he wipes tables. He was born with a soundtrack in his heart and is never scared to let the world see him enjoy it.

The sound of his movements is drowned out by the music, allowing him to sneak up behind me and grab my sudsy hands just to spin me around, pulling me into his performance.

I want to kiss him. The thought slams into me.

I want to pop up on my toes and add one more note of perfection. But if I do that, I might break this spell. I will do anything to keep basking in the light that is Bennett. I'll bury the growing desire for more if I can preserve this.

"I can't tell you how much it means that you came with me to help," he says as we leave.

"I was just feeling really motivated to repay the free coffees."

"Don't mention that to my mom."

"I'll take it to my grave," I promise. I'll never say anything to Diane. She so incredibly overflows with love that she can't help but share it. I don't want to dim the things she did out of love by making them transactional.

This had been far better than any day laying on the sand reading.

When Diane realized my birthday was in December a couple of years ago, she started to buy me a gift for my half-birthday. She said she didn't want to ship it to me because the best part of giving a gift is seeing the person's reaction. Last year, she got me a signed copy of *Murder on the Orient Express*, and the year before, it was a swimsuit I had pointed out in a boutique that makes me feel like a mermaid every time I wear it.

I take what looks like a board game out of an iridescent gift bag.

"It's a cold case. They give you all the clues, and you decide who to arrest. It's just like all your mystery books," she says.

I have never been good at solving the ones in books, but it's worth a shot. Nothing can happen if I accuse the wrong fictional character.

"I was so jealous when Mom said that wasn't for us. Promise you won't do it without me," Bennett begs.

"Ok, Detective Sorenson, I won't even take a peek." I hold out my hand to seal the promise.

Three days later, it's pouring. It isn't the type of rain you can dance in, enjoying the coolness as it seeps through clothes and drenches hair. No, this is the type with violent drops falling so fast they sting a little bit when they hit you. Perfect weather for solving a mystery.

Bennett braves the fifty feet between our houses. Mom was off on a day trip to an alpaca farm. Or maybe that was last week, and she's doing a pottery intensive. I'm unsure why she needs a full weekend for either of those, but it means the house is empty.

"I've brought provisions." He holds up a bag holding frozen pizza and hot chocolate mix.

"I'll get the oven ready and heat some milk."

"Absolutely not. I am a professional beverage creator, and unless you've forgotten, you're still in training. There is a wrong way and a right way to make hot cocoa, and I would bet good money that you can't tell me the difference."

"Isn't the wrong way just using water instead of milk?" I'm bad in the kitchen, but I at least know that.

"Watch and learn," he says.

He sifts through the cabinets, pulling out vanilla, cinnamon, and marshmallows.

I watch as he heats the milk I set out and throws in dashes of cinnamon and a splash of vanilla.

"If you had just told me, I could have done everything myself. I don't see why you had to make it," I protest, even though the drinks are already being poured into mugs. I always wish we had fun touristy mugs with cartoon renderings of the beach, but instead, we have a plain set in a deep blue.

"I had to add the secret ingredient."

"I swear if you say, love, I will shove you right out back into the rain-" I say just as he finishes his thought.

"Love."

I attempt to wrestle him to the door, but I can't even move him out of the kitchen. He's solid as I shove against his chest. Breathless, I looked up at his smug face.

"Don't talk shit about my recipe until you try it," he says.

I snatch the mug from him and sip the steaming chocolate. He's right, just like he has been about all his drink creations. I preheat the oven for the pizza, and we head to the living room.

"Now, for the real reason I'm here." He walks over to the entertainment console to grab the cold case game. "I have waited months to play this. I swear Mom would leave it on the counter just to taunt me."

"I see. You had a hidden agenda, lulling me into complacency with sweet drinks and company."

"I am a gentleman; I would do no such thing." He fakes a wounded expression holding his hand over his heart. We lay out the contents of the box on the coffee table. It's an assortment of fake documents and papers curated to tell the story of a murdered heiress.

Bennett is inspecting the direction pamphlet, "Let's make this a game."

"It's already a game."

"You know what I mean. Let's see who can solve it first." I want to tell him that I need his help to solve this, that I'm no good at sifting through clues. I'm a person meant to read mysteries, not solve them. But I can't say no to the twinkle in his eye. After all, these things are designed to be solved. From the age range on the box, they expect fourteen-year-olds to have a fair chance of figuring it out.

"Ok, but what do I get when I win?" I ask, laying on a thick layer of false confidence.

"You'll just have to wait and see." He claims a stack of papers and a notebook.

I sort through the remaining documents and pull out a newspaper clipping. Scarlet Valentine, yes, that was the name they chose, was the heiress to a diamond empire. She was found dead the morning before the company announced she was taking her father's position. The coroner's report says that it was poison.

The only people who knew about the will were the interim CEO, her father's best friend. Scarlet's bodyguard, her secret lover. Her stepmother. And her assistant. Each profile had been designed to be suspicious, with fragmented alibis and plausible motives.

As I inspect the papers I've collected, I go in circles. I lean into a gut feeling that it was the assistant. She is the least likely, so I'm even more apprehensive about why she's in the mix. When I lean back, I glimpse something under the couch.

"Cheater!" I call out, breaking the silence as I grab the document near Bennett's feet.

"That is a wild accusation, Detective Danes," he says, trying to snatch the paper from my hands. I duck under his arm and run around the couch to put a barrier between us as I scan what he was hiding. The paper makes my line of reasoning click into place.

It's a paternity test for the assistant that proves that she was the half-sister of the dead heiress. Which means the assistant is next in line to inherit everything.

"I've got it. I win!" I'm practically jumping up and down.

"Not so fast. I have just finished building my own case."

"I guess whoever figured it out wins." I've never been nearly as competitive as him, but I am determined to win this time.

"Ok, present your case to the jury."

"It was the assistant. She came to the city from the middle of nowhere to seek out Scarlet less than a year before her murder. She was trying to find her half-sister. And this paternity test." I wave the paper in my hand, "This proves that they are related. The assistant killed Scarlet to take over the fortune as the last remaining descendent on the father's side. She would have plenty of means because she had access to Scarlet's schedule and location at all times." I'm proud of what I figured out until Bennett starts.

"You've got it all wrong. That's all pure speculation. It was the stepmom. This is the amended will." He holds up a paper just like I had, "It says that if his children are no longer alive at the time the will is executed, his fortune falls to the wife. And there is no evidence that she knew the assistant was a long lost daughter. Also, her alibi has a two hour gap, right when Scarlet was supposed to have been poisoned. Your suspect was at a gala that entire night and was spotted frequently throughout the night."

"Well, we won't know until we open the last envelope." The last document is sealed and will reveal if we have succeeded at our task.

We huddle together, opening up the folded pages. We read in silence, taking in its contents.

"You're kidding me," he grumbles. As it turns out, we are both wrong.

"It really is always the boyfriend, or I guess, in this case, husband." The bodyguard and the heiress had gotten secretly married days before. Despite the video footage of him standing outside of her room the entire evening and morning, he had slipped poison into her room service coffee. Somewhere in the pile are security pictures of him with the coffee. "I guess we both lost."

"Yeah, this sucks. I was really looking forward to winning." He turns to me. His thigh brushes against mine. My eyes fix on where we're touching. I attempt to steady my breath. The rain and his proximity are making my head dizzy. I should pull away. I should go get more hot chocolate. But I can't convince my legs to move.

"You never told me what the prize was." I meet his eyes. We're nearly nose to nose.

"This." He closes the gap between us and presses his lips against mine.

I pause, letting my mind register that this isn't a dream. I have to convince myself that I didn't just conjure this up from wanting it so badly. I'm fully awake, and Bennett Sorenson is kissing me.

My hands find his back and pull him in as close as possible. I could live a thousand lives in this moment, tucked away with him, the rain crashing down around the house, isolating us from the rest of the world.

We only pull apart when a deafening crack of thunder rings out.

It isn't my first kiss, which belongs to Michael in seventh grade after a school dance. There were a few more kisses and things with other boys that went further, but none of them were Bennett.

This is the first kiss that matters, a kiss to measure all future kisses against.

His eyes search my face, "I've been wanting to do that for so long."

"I've been too scared to ask you too." I reach up to hold his face in my hands. There is no more guessing, hopelessly attempting to untangle the meaning behind his touch and stares. "What about Nicole?" The question escapes before I can stop it.

He jerks back, "What does Nicole have to do with this?"

"I just thought that you two had something going on. That maybe you didn't want to tell me for some reason. You were just getting along so well, and she's like model gorgeous," I'm rambling, rattling off all of the anxieties that have been building up over the first month back. I had texted them all to Cammie, but no one was here to actually say this stuff to.

It's not like I could have gone up to Tanner to ask *Sorry, I turned you down last year. By the way, is your brother dating anyone?*

"Whoa, slow down. Nicole and I are just friends. Even if she wanted that to be different, you are the only person I look at that way. It's been you for so damn long. I can't explain what you've done to me these last few years. After that first year, summer only starts when you get here." He's holding my face rubbing away a tear that I don't remember falling. His touch is grounding, helping oxygen reenter my lungs. He kisses my nose and pulls back.

"There's no summer without you for me either," I say.

"Good. I was starting to think my obsession with you was one sided."

We spent the rest of the day curled around each other. We forget about the pizza until I go into the kitchen to grab water and see the preheated oven. The storm makes us feel like the only people on the beach, in our own bubble of happiness.

I already thought that we were inseparable before. Now, there is time for nothing else but him.

Every day becomes a cycle of running from the café into the water and then to my house to become tangled in each other. His kisses taste like coffee in the morning and like the ocean in the afternoon.

We keep things between us for the first week. It's like we were in on a huge secret. At his house, he pulls me around corners into a kiss or holds my hand under the blanket while watching movies with Tanner and his parents. I like having this version of us all to myself.

Even though she's not at the beach, I don't tell Cammie. I like the secret, but also telling other people makes it more real. Making something real means risking it falling apart. I don't doubt what I feel for Bennett. But feelings this consuming terrify me. I don't know how to contain them.

Our secret finally slips at dinner one night when Tanner drops his fork and notices our interlaced fingers under the table when he bends to pick it up.

"Finally!" Tanner nearly knocks his head as he sits up. I start to pull away, but Bennett squeezes my hand in reassurance. "I thought I was going to have to suffer through another summer of him sighing every time you walked by in a swimsuit." I blush. "You know he always looks like a sad puppy the day you leave? He just mopes around and reads whatever books you've left behind." My heart flutters, learning that he does practically the same things I do.

Diane playfully hits her middle child with a dish towel on her way back from the kitchen. "Don't embarrass them, or we'll have to wait another three years." She gives me a smile, "I'm happy you finally made the move on our Emma. I was also tired of waiting."

"How do you know it was me? For all you know, she jumped me for a kiss and professed her undying love!" Everyone trades glances and breaks into fits of laughter. It's not like I hadn't considered it, but he's the brave one.

A heat advisory drives us inside during the stickiest part of the day. The type of scorching, humid air that even submerging in the ocean can't provide complete relief from. Bennett and I are hiding at my place, cranking up the AC and stealing kisses as we watch sitcom reruns.

It doesn't take long until we grow to progressively needier touches. I'm on his lap, pressed against him. His hand runs up and down my leg. Each touch makes my stomach dance. Before long, our shirts lay discarded. This is the point where we usually stop or get interrupted. I don't want to stop, and from the feeling beneath me, he doesn't want to either.

"I want all of you. Do you want that too?" He asks, looking up into my eyes. I stare back into liquid pools of amber and dive in.

"Yes." I kiss him softly on his jaw, my lips grazing the barest hint of stubble.

"Will this be your first time?" He cups my cheek, and I lean into the soft touch.

"No," I say like a confession. We didn't really talk about the people we had met between summers. I had never told him that I had sex for the first time after Sophomore year Homecoming. Harvey Young and I had gone together, and it felt like the right thing to do. Despite the fact that it was terrible and awkward, I don't regret doing it. "But this will be the first time with someone I care about."

"It's mine. It's always been you for me. It never felt right to be with anyone else." He must see the guilt flash across my face. "I don't care that you have been with other people before. I don't need to be your first. I just want to be the last person for you." I want that too.

I'm relieved he hadn't built up this moment for us together. If he had, I wouldn't have been able to give that to him, and I want to give him everything.

The movements are less sloppy than my first time, but still hesitant. We move like any wrong touch could hurt the other, despite the ferocity of everything we'd done leading up to this. It isn't perfect; the best things aren't.

Girls at school had talked about how it was normal for sex to be better for the guy the first couple of times. I don't reach the same euphoria as Bennett, but I can tell we are going in the right direction.

"Sometimes I think I was born just to spend summers with you," he whispers. His hand tucks a curl behind my ear. Somehow, whenever he does it, they stay in place, molding to his touch as much as the rest of my body.

"I want to spend every single one of mine with you," I say.

The second most important development of the summer is that Tanner finally got his boating license. The Sorensons have a boat that's been largely unused and had needed repairs. Tanner spent every day until his 19th birthday making sure it was seaworthy. We pack sandwiches and beers tucked in the corners of the cooler that can only be noticed if someone makes a close inspection.

The wind whips my hair behind me as the shore becomes a distant speck. The subtle rocking of the boat is foreign and has me bracing against the edge, taking deep breaths, slamming my eyes shut to steady myself. This is what people probably mean by getting their sea legs. I will adjust, I repeat to myself. I hear the rustling of the guys and their muttering about bait and fishing rods. Still, I can't open my eyes. We're set in one place, but my stomach still does somersaults. I sit, listening to the swish of the fishing line. I don't know how long this continues before I hear the cooler crack open.

"Anyone want lunch?" These word break whatever control I had over my body. I lurch to the side, expelling the contents of my stomach. As I crumple to the floor, a form blocks the sun as I curl into myself, too aware of the gentle movements of the water.

"Hey, are you ok?" I know it's redundant, and I can't answer even if it isn't. Who loses their breakfast and is ok? A hand makes soft circles on my back. The conversation above me consists of shouts about getting back home and packing up.

Diane meets us at the dock. The boys must have called her on the way back. She shoves a small glass into my hands and tells me to drink. I do, and the taste of ginger burns down my throat. I cough after finishing the entire thing, and it feels like I'm about to breathe fire.

"I think I'll stay on land from now on," I say, and everyone chuckles.

From then on, I see the boys off on the days they go fishing or just want to be on the water. Diane never goes with them either, insistent that she needs to be available for emergencies at Early Bird. I'm not sure what type of emergencies can take place at a café, but I don't question it because it means I have company while everyone else is away.

She teaches me how to make different pastries. We get coated in clouds of flour, and when it comes to cleaning up, we stand back and wonder how the brownie batter got on the ceiling.

Each day, she shows me some tricks, like how to get a cake to not stick to the pan and the perfect amount of sugar to help yeast bloom. I learn that orange zest is a magic ingredient for so many recipes.

She helps me make my own batches of muffins and cookies, but they never turn out as good. Still, it makes me more confident that I won't be entirely reliant on Bennett for making meals when I get to Portland.

I have also become her official taste tester when she tries new flavor combinations for muffins and scones.

"I'm not sure that cayenne pepper belongs in these." I'm coughing between sips of water. The heat of the muffin is making me burn from the inside out.

"Hmmm, maybe I'll cut the amount in half," she says to herself. Just then, the boys climb into the house, perfectly sun kissed and windswept.

"Your mom is trying to poison me."

"I don't think Mom does anything half-assed. If she wanted to poison you via dessert, you'd be long gone." Bennett tells me.

Diane hadn't been blind to what all the time we spent sneaking off meant. She, Bennett, Tanner, and I are all sitting on the porch on a Sunday morning when this becomes embarrassingly clear.

"I just hope you're being safe. I don't plan on having grandchildren until either Jones settles down or everyone here is thoroughly educated," she says in a tone too casual for what she just spoke out into the world.

Tanner and I choke on the coffee we are inhaling with various degrees of grace. Mine makes its way down my throat. Tanner is unfortunate enough to be the first person I've seen to have coffee come out of their nose. I bet it stings like a bitch, but it is probably some form of karma. To his credit, Bennett is unphased, as if he'd been expecting to talk about our sex life at nine in the morning.

"Don't worry, we have condoms, and Emma got an IUD last fall," Bennett tells her, practically waving off the question. My jaw falls open. *He could have just said We're using protection*, Mom. No, he had to explain exactly what we'd been using.

"Good," Diane says, going back to sipping her coffee.

Tanner and I exchange glances translating to *Did we both just experience the most chill sex talk in the history of the universe?* I'm just happy Richard isn't here to add his two cents.

My mom's reaction is far less pleasant.

Bennett and I are on the couch watching TV when she returns from whatever excursion she had been off to this week, a vineyard trip, from what the last text says. His arm is slung around my shoulders, and our hands are interlaced on my lap.

We've spent more time at my house this summer than any other year. Partly because it is the best way to avoid potentially scarring run-ins with his family. But also, because when he's here, it feels like the home I've been dreaming it would become.

"Emma, can you help me bring my bag upstairs?" my mother asks. She looks over at Bennett as if she finally realizes he's there. "Oh, hello, Bennett. I have to steal Emma for the rest of the day. Tell Mrs. Sorenson I say hello." She never calls Diane by her first name; it's always Mrs. Sorenson or Bennett's mother.

Bennett moves to leave at her dismissal.

I give him a quick peck, "I'll see you later."

My mother claiming to need me for the rest of the day is the first sign things are off. Our lives at the beach didn't overlap. We never spend more than a few hours together each day. An entire afternoon is unheard of.

I follow her upstairs, carrying her overnight bag, which has no right to be so heavy. In her room, she sets down her phone-sized purse on the vanity and turns my way with a huff, "I thought you had started to think about your future."

"I am." I told her my plan to go to Portland. It's one of the East Coast's top-rated schools, but she told me I had to 'cast a wider net.' I added the Ivies to my list because she asked, even though I don't have the extracurriculars or advanced courses for even chance of admission, and also added a couple of schools in Virginia.

"College isn't the only thing you need to start thinking about at your age. You're about to be an adult. These next few years will determine everything." She sifts through her purse to pull out a light nude lipstick. "Corrina warned me this might happen with those boys next door."

"You're talking about my relationship with Bennett? We're being safe, if that's what you mean," I ask, a pit forming in my stomach. I'm realizing she's not concerned with that part of my future.

She's never said anything negative about him or our friendship. He had always been a 'nice boy,' and when I mentioned that he helps at the café, she even said she admired his hard work.

"You're not sixteen anymore. It's fine to run around the beach and forget about the future when you're young, but you're almost an adult. You need to start looking for someone to help you be something in this world." At her words, I attempt to center myself. Bennett makes me happy isn't that all I should care about? But that's not what she means. She means the type of person with connections, like the sons of my dad's coworkers, and future hedge fund managers.

"I'm serious about him. He's going to law school if you're worried about that."

"You know how many people say they're going to go into law and change direction in the first year or don't get accepted? Trust me, I know from experience." The thought of my mother ever attempting to study law or strive beyond the title of doting philanthropist is a startling image. "What happens when he takes on loans and doesn't make money until after seven years of school? You're missing the implications of your actions. You think you have all the time in the world, but it will catch up to you faster than you expect."

The idea of what we'll look like in eight years is dizzying. We've only known each other for just under half of that. We've only been officially together for a month. What if we can't make it past a year?

"None of that matters."

"Whatever you need to believe. We all have our little flings. Enjoy it while it lasts." She turns from me, done with the conversation. Apparently, the boys next door are good enough to be fun, but they have no place in our lives outside of Harriettesville.

I want to storm out and slam the door, but that won't win this fight. The best I can do is prove her wrong. The force that has drawn Bennett and me together over the years is stronger than her elitist bullshit.

Each time I'm in Bennett's room, I discover something new. Since the book sale last year, he's gotten more into reading. The books on his shelf are either ones I give him once I'm finished or nonfiction about the ocean. Not the cute picture encyclopedias and fun fact books you get gifted as a kid. No, these are about climate change and coral reefs or deep sea creatures that are guaranteed to give you nightmares.

I brush my finger along the spines as I read the titles. "You've read all of these?" I'm impressed. Everyone tells me I'm a reader when I come to the beach, but I never read anything like this. Books that mean something.

"All but the ones on my desk." He points to a small stack.

"They're all so dense."

"It's easy to want to learn everything about what you care about."

I sit next to him on the bed. "I can't wait to see you save the world." I mean it. When Bennett talks about the ocean, he lights up.

"I don't know about saving the world, but I'll settle for protecting the parts of it that I love."

"Just take me along with you when you do." I kiss him.

"I wouldn't do it with anyone else," I add this to our ever growing list of things we have in store for our future.

"Good."

I want him to be my future. I want summer to last forever until we're old and grey. Until we get to see two people meet on the beach just like we did.

Here in his arms, I know one thing for sure, "I think I'm in love with you, Bennett Sorenson." I don't just love him. I'm consumed by every part of him. Every once in a while, I get lost in the reality that he's chosen to direct the sunlight that pours out of him on me. While he is the sun, I'm happy to be stuck in his gravitational pull, lost in orbit.

"I think I'm in love with you too, Emma Danes."

This summer is the hardest to leave, after Bennett and I finally confirmed the tender thing growing between us. Now that we have it driving home makes it feel less real. Each mile between me and the beach is one more step into my other life, a world untouched by the magic he's brought me.

11
Fall
Five year ago

The distance becomes a doorway for my mother's words to creep in. Without Cammie's constant reassurance and weekly calls with Bennett, I'd be spiraling.

With college talk picking up more, I feel nothing but lost. I flip through the Portland catalog and see hundreds of majors. How will I know which one is right? It would take years to try out different departments and concentrations. My lack of direction becomes my biggest obstacle when writing admission essays. Each question is nightmare fuel. Why do you want to come to this university? What are your plans for the future? What goals do you have for college?

When I tell Bennett and Cammie I'm struggling to write my essays, they send me theirs. None of it helps. If anything, it's worse seeing how they talk about their passions. Cammie wrote about how going to Europe for college will help her be immersed in the birthplace of so many artists and help her understand the history of the art that she hopes to restore. While Bennett talked about living on the water and how he used to take it for granted until he learned about environmental threats that might destroy the natural beauty of his home.

The best I can come up with is imagining what it might be like to be there. Moving somewhere new after living in one place my entire life. I talk about learning through exploration and the ability to do so in a city rich in history and art. My advisor says what I already know, it lacks direction.

I take the ACT one last time. My new score helps to supplement the weaker parts of my application.

I text Bennett a picture of my email from Portland saying they've received my application. We celebrate with a long phone call while I drink a stolen glass of my mother's wine. I try not to think about what might happen to us if I don't get in.

In early December, I get a box from Bennett. The box is a couple of inches thick but as big as my desk. It's so light that I could easily toss it in the air despite its size.

I have no idea what it could be. My birthday is in a few weeks, but I'll be going to Harriettesville. There's no reason he would need to send me anything.

I'm careful when I cut through the tape. Opening the flaps to reveal a ton of shredded colored paper with a little note placed on top.

Call me with your answer.

I brush away the paper to show a poster board that says, "*I Want To Sea You at Prom.*" Prom is spelled out with tiny seashells. It's so cheesy, but it's perfect.

"Hey. What's your answer?" He picks up.

"How do you know what I'm calling about?"

"I had notifications on to see when it got delivered."

"Yes, Bennett Sorenson. I want to *sea* you at prom too."

"God, I'm so lucky."

"I'm the lucky one who gets to have their hot college boyfriend there."

"Emma Danes, you think I'm hot? How scandalous."

"No, I must be thinking of another Sorenson boy. How's Jones these days?"

We talk until his next class.

He's been sending me pictures of his walk to class. The campus is a forest of trees and old Gothic chapel like buildings. Because there are classes all freshmen are required to take, he gives me reviews of the professors, which ones are funny or bad at replying to emails.

The only pictures I don't love are the ones he sends when he's out with friends. Maybe it's because I wish I was there with him, or I'm reading too much into the girls in some of them; his arm slung over their shoulders. I don't like that I don't trust him completely. I have to shove down the thought that he might find someone more like him and realize I'm not worth waiting for.

These thoughts always make me feel guilty the next day when he sends me a good morning text.

I have to keep reminding myself *soon*. Soon I'll drive up for my birthday. Then soon, I'll be there for the entire summer. And soon after that, we won't have to spend days apart.

We'll have a hundred summers. And every day between.

I just need to get into college first.

12

Thursday

Now

We are trapped inside by the storm. The whipping rain and crashes of thunder create an ominous energy. We force Josh to watch another horror movie. This one is a found footage film set on a boat in the Bermuda Triangle. Each time there is a clap of thunder, he makes a squeaking noise. Just as the movie ends, a loud tapping starts on the glass of the sliding door. Everyone in the room sits up a little straighter. But it's just Jordan, Theo, and Bennett.

"Did we just walk in on something?" Jordan comments on our shocked expressions. In our defense, the movie was pretty fucked up and had everyone on edge. We must have looked cultish with only the light from the screen illuminating our faces.

"No, everything's fine." Caleb's voice is pitched a little higher than usual. Jordan still looks suspicious.

"We brought some hot chocolate and stuff for hot toddies if anyone wants something stronger," Bennett says, holding up a plastic bag. I've played out this scene before: the boy, the hot chocolate, and the rain.

We get up from the couch, shaking off the horror induced adrenaline rush.

As Bennett reaches the kitchen, I'm already hunting for cinnamon and vanilla that aren't there. Bennett must have predicted this because he's brought his own. I can't read his expression when he looks over at me as I close the cabinet. I didn't think before looking for the ingredients, old habits die hard.

We have so many memories tied to stormy days in this house.

"Looking for something?" He quirks up an eyebrow.

"No nothing." As I pass by to leave, I tell him, "Don't hurt yourself by putting extra love in my hot chocolate."

"I won't," he mutters as I walk away.

I join the others who are sorting through some tattered looking board games in the entertainment console. Bennett is in full barista mode, bringing out drinks for everyone and insisting he doesn't need help.

My mind flashes to what it would be like if we were all here on different terms. If we were hosting our friends together at the beach. I can picture it so clearly.

I can tell they all like him and the guys. I just wish I could enjoy it more.

"I'm bored. And these games suck," Libby whines, but she's right. Most of the games are missing enough pieces that they're nearly impossible to play. The one puzzle is missing an entire edge worth of pieces. We started

Monopoly after hunting down a paper clip and a small shell to replace the missing game pieces, but we stopped when we realized there wasn't enough money to play with. We ran into similar issues with the other games that could accommodate most of the group.

"Let's play sardines," Amber says from Josh's lap.

"What?"

"Sardines? The game where one person hides, and people hide with them until no one else is looking." She mistakes my confusion at the suggestion for not knowing what it was. Crawling into a tight space with everyone else, particularly the man with the amber eyes staring directly at me, is a terrible scenario. But I'm immediately outvoted.

"No, that's a great idea. The only one that knows this house is Emma, so she should start," Jess reminds everyone. Great idea.

"You have one minute to hide." Theo has a timer pulled up on his phone and starts it before I'm even on my feet.

Everyone closes their eyes and turns away as I sprint for the stairs. I know the perfect spot. In what used to be my old closet, there is a little alcove at the far end for extra storage. I used to store my books and suitcases there. It can probably fit four or five people before people will have to hide in the main part of the closet.

I have to move quickly to pull the heavy dresser blocking the entrance away from the wall. Thankfully, the new owners don't use the space for storage, so it's empty. I'm struggling to pull the dresser back in place just as the beeping of Theo's timer rings out.

I'm panting from exertion as I settle into the unlit space. What is that dresser made of? I attempt to calm my breath as I hear someone enter the room. They open the closet but only give it a quick look. Three more people repeat this before I start to see the dresser shift.

I had forgotten something important: Bennett also knows this house fairly well. I can feel my pulse racing as he ducks down to find me and crawls into the space. He replaces the dresser with much more ease than I did.

He has the option to take the space across from me but chooses the spot next to me instead. I'm closed in between him and the wall. His legs bump into mine as he pulls them to his chest. This is the first time we've been completely alone for days.

I want to say something, but he presses his finger to my lips as another set of footsteps enters the room. I don't think I'm breathing. His touch on my lips causes fire to flow through my veins, dissipating the chill of the tiny space. When he lowers his hand, it brushes my thigh in a way I'm not sure is unintentional. I suck in the sound that is about to escape my lips.

Those small touches ignite me more than anyone I'd been with throughout college. But he doesn't stop torturing me.

"Did you have something to say just now?" He leans in, whispering in my ear so I can feel his breath on my neck. I have nowhere to shift to as his legs press against mine.

"No," I squeak.

Just then, the closet door opens someone moves the dresser. Caleb pops his head in.

"Just because the game is called Sardines doesn't mean you have to cram yourselves in there so tight," he whispers.

Soon enough, Theo and Jess also discover the alcove, which actually necessitates squeezing together in the tight space. When Amber attempts to crawl in, there is officially no more room.

Instead of trying to coordinate efforts, Bennett hauls me onto his lap. My back is pressed against his chest. I try to keep some distance between us, but his arm is around my waist, gluing me to him while his other hand covers my mouth so I can't make a startled sound.

I'm thankful for the darkness so no one else can see how red my cheeks must be. For a second, he squeezes his arm tighter around me, inclining his head in challenge.

What are you going to do, Emma?

"Good idea, man," Caleb says. He motions for Jess to crawl onto his lap.

I can't even appreciate that Caleb has finally made some semblance of a move. Instead, all my senses are directed to the hard chest that I'm pinned to. I glare up at Bennett and can tell that he sees by the silent laugh that rolls through him. Jordan is next to slide in, and he can't quite get the dresser flush with the wall.

My mind wanders to fixating on how close Bennett's lips are to mine. If either of us shifts, we'll be kissing. Will those lips still taste the same if I move closer?

I hope they do.

I'm not sure how long I'm stuck like this, pressed into him. It felt like it's been hours, but it's likely only minutes before Josh and Libby find us, apparently having teamed up once the rest of us disappeared.

"I swear I checked this closet so many times," Libby says, looking as if we are all rabbits jumping out of a hat.

Josh looks defeated, "I agree. There's no way this was here before."

"Yeah, the house created a little pocket universe that only the rest of us could find," Caleb says.

The group starts the awkward process of crawling or hunching over to leave. Bennett and I are in the farthest corner. I'm trapped in here until everyone is out. When there's finally enough space to get up, I attempt to move. Bennett's arm is still like iron as he holds me to him.

I push off him. "Was that really necessary?" I hiss, not wanting anyone lingering nearby to hear.

"I think so." He gives me a wink as I catch my breath. After all this time, he still has so much power over me.

It's just the rain and this house. When the sun comes out, he'll be an ass again, and I can stop wanting him. But I wanted him last night too, and it wasn't raining this hard then.

Everyone has already headed back downstairs for drinks. I stand at the top of the stairs processing what just happened. He has successfully made me lose my mind.

Looking out the window, the rain hasn't let up. If anything, it's heavier, falling in grape sized drops. When Theo suggests another horror movie, Josh turns a shade of white that has the rest of us catch our laughs and nearly spit out our drinks.

"You know I'd be happy with sunflowers and rainbows for once," Josh says.

"That sounds like a children's show," Theo comments, already hunting through the horror section.

"What's wrong with children's shows?" Jordan looks mildly offended.

Amber sighs, "Give him a break. I'm going to wear him out plenty later tonight."

"You didn't just say that." Libby snorts.

"Oh yes, I did. Get your earplugs ready." Amber gets an awkward amount of horny whenever she defends Josh's honor. Her affection takes the reigns in a way that promises to make everyone uncomfortable.

"Moving past that nice little bit of unsolicited information, what about a good old fashioned romcom?" Theo asks. "No guts or gore guaranteed."

He selects a small town romance that shares an unbearable amount of similarities to Bennett's and my relationship.

She comes into town, and he's the first person she meets. Check.

He makes her feel like part of his family. Check.

They mess everything up, ending with tears and broken hearts. Check.

The only difference is they end up happy, and we're- I don't know what we are, but we never got a happily ever after with a cute apartment and family holidays.

Horror movies maybe be Josh's downfall, but this cute, feel-good movie may be the end of me.

We have three more days here. I thought the last time I left; it would be forever.

I want another summer. The thought is a betrayal. I don't want another summer with how things are. I want to go back to who we were four years ago.

But if wanting was all it took to make things happen, my heart would stop aching.

I had wanted Bennett.

In an entirely different way, I wanted Jackson.

Now I just want to stop feeling.

It's spring break. Spring break is fun and full of stupid mistakes that you're supposed to joke about after graduation.

As the couple on the screen whispers, 'I love you' and kisses, I can't take it anymore. I head to the kitchen with the excuse of grabbing more popcorn. I must have accidentally turned my phone on because it won't stop dinging from my back pocket. The only reason I know my mother won't come down here herself is that she has her own demons in Harriettesville she wants to avoid.

"Is that Jackson? Is he finally begging?" Libby says, twisting open a beer.

"No, still nothing." We've been so busy that I don't think of him often. But each time his name comes up, it's like poking a fresh wound.

"Ok. If you need to talk about it, let me know. Who's blowing up your phone then?"

"Just my mom," I wince. They all know how rocky my relationship with my parents is.

"I'm sorry."

"I'll be fine. I didn't mean to bring down the vibe with my shit." I make sure to say in a playful tone as she heads back to the couch.

Bennett must have been eavesdropping, "Why do you keep doing that?"

"Doing what?"

"Making sure they are having a good trip even if you're hurting and stressed. You keep talking about *their* last spring break together. What about yours? Don't you also deserve that? You talk like everyone else is supposed to be here, like they just let you in on accident."

"I'm fine," I snap. Each time I say it, I'm less sure.

"Don't lie to me. They can read you pretty well, but I have memorized every part of you."

"Haven't we already established I'm here because my boyfriend broke up with me?"

"I've known Libby and Amber for less than four days, and they don't seem like they would keep people around just to make them feel better." He's right. The others can get along with anyone but not Libby or Amber. I've seen Amber block someone for spelling her last name wrong over text.

"I'm just lucky. I don't deserve them putting up with me." It had been luck. Each of them came into my life at random. Now they all have bright futures, and I've continued to plateau.

"How long will it take for you to see how special you are?" He does a lap around the kitchen island. "God, I want to shake you right now. You used to always say that this place made you special. Why can't it go both ways? I spent so many summers here, and you're the one thing that made me count down the days until June."

"You've got it all wrong."

"How?"

How? I wasn't anybody until I came here. He was the igniting force that helped me become somebody. He helped to form me into someone other than who my parents planned for me to be. He had dragged me into existence.

"I met you and Diane and Tanner. You all completed me. I'm who I am because you let me in. I would still be that girl who couldn't get in the water if I never met you. If you want to say anyone deserves to be out there with them, it's you. You and the guys made this trip so much more special than it would have been without you." I pause before I say, "I'm happy you didn't leave me alone." These words come from the deepest part of me. I know the same pieces of me that my friends like are the ones that he gave me.

"You are so much more than that. You were never incomplete, scared maybe, but not incomplete." He's stopped pacing around the room.

"Tell me who I was without you," I demand.

It only takes him a couple of strides before I'm pressed between him in the counter. "You're impossible. You've given everyone you've ever met a chance. You listen like every word someone says is the most important thing you've ever heard. You're scared, but you don't let that control you. Those things have nothing to do with me." He's inches from me, lifting my chin so I can no longer avert my gaze. This feels more intimate than when he held me in the closet. "I don't love you for no reason. Give me some credit."

The air seems to rush out of the room at his final words. As if realizing what he's said, he leaves.

It takes me a minute to process that he's said love, not loved. Everything else he's said until now seemed like the bitter remnants of feelings. His slip gives my mind permission to admit what I've been hiding from this entire time. I don't go back to everyone until I'm sure I won't cry.

Even after trying to cleanse the evening with a scorching hot shower, I can't sleep.

After lying next to Jess for as long as I can manage, I creep downstairs, leaving through the front door so I don't wake up Libby.

A haze of mist makes the sand cloud-like like I'm hovering between a dream and wakefulness.

The air is heavy with humidity from the deluge. I my hair is still damp from the shower; I can see it start to curl in the way it only does at the beach.

Nighttime on the beach is the perfect place for lying. For spinning fantasies. We don't acknowledge how often we lie to ourselves to make life more barrable. We only think of lies as betrayals, not the soft things that we use to survive.

With one word, Bennett cracked the foundation of a life I had built on a lie. Four years of empty promises, swearing that I didn't love him anymore. Convincing myself that it was meant to fall apart.

I tell myself one last lie.

We never fell apart that winter. He's waiting inside for me; all I have to do is walk through the door and return to him.

13

Winter

Five years ago

I drive the six hours to Harriettesville by myself for the first time. My shiny new powder blue convertible is a pre-college birthday gift. I'm completely in control of the trip. It's all on my terms. Because it's my birthday, my mother doesn't protest or make any passing comments about the trip. Everything's falling in place for the perfect weekend. One thing stays on repeat in my head: Bennett Sorenson.

His lips.

His hands.

Him. Escaping into those thoughts makes the drive fly by.

I texted him when I reached the town limits, so it's no surprise to find him sitting on the porch waiting for me. The moment I step out of the car, his arms are around me.

For one month, we're the same age. I won't be able to celebrate with him in February because we'll both be in school, but I have his present already wrapped under my bed. An old nautical guide with gilded edges and an embossed cover.

"Happy Birthday." His face settles into the crook of my neck, planting a kiss. I wasn't sure what I expected of him in a Harriettesville winter. He is in a Portland sweatshirt, faded jeans, and house slippers a few sizes too small. He's wearing rings, which he never did in the summer because he was worried the water would make them tarnish.

In the past, my parents always insisted on throwing a party for me. It was always their party, just with my name on it. They would invite their coworkers and people mom knew from charity work. There was always some theme that could have been used for a Homecoming dance like 'Night Under the Stars.'

Bennett has promised the perfect party but insists on everything being a surprise. The only thing he's relented on is telling me that no one is dressing up, so I only should if I want to.

"Let me help you get unloaded, and then I have to run back to the house to finish some stuff up." I only have one bag for the weekend, but he claims it's his duty to bring it inside.

The house is more echoey in the winter, almost as if the summer sun filled part of it up. I hurry to throw everything where it belongs and change out of my road trip sweats. I want to get out of here and into the inviting light of the Sorenson house.

It is nearly a week after Christmas, but their tree is still up. Most of the ornaments are homemade. Sand dollars strung up with ribbon, little pipe cleaner palm trees. At the top of the tree is a starfish.

I approach the kitchen but don't move closer once I hear a hushed argument.

"You've known for months. Why won't you tell her?" Tanner asks.

"I'll tell her tomorrow. I don't want to ruin her birthday, and what's one more day? I know I should have said something sooner, but it was our last real summer together before college, and she was so happy."

"Bennett, there's no such thing as a perfect time to tell anyone something like this. You've been putting it off too long. You're eighteen. It's time to stop pretending. Stop shielding her from the world; you aren't kids anymore." With Tanner's last words, I hear someone moving toward where I'm lingering.

I know one thing for certain. I was not supposed to hear that conversation. I'm trapped between two options: confess I overheard them and confront whatever truth they are hiding, or trust him to tell me.

I trust him. That's what we do.

Bennett comes around the corner and pulls me into a kiss, "Hey, you got ready so fast."

"Yeah, I'm just so excited." I look up at him.

"Follow me." He takes my hand. We go out the front and around the house. It becomes apparent we're going in a circle to the deck.

"Why didn't we just go through the back?"

"Because that would ruin the effect."

As I take in the deck, I can't do anything to stifle my gasp. He was right. It is perfect. They've replicated Diane's birthday from that first summer. Strings of lights are wrapped around every available surface. The cake is the same design but has a lemon blueberry filling instead of vanilla. A paper banner has 'Happy 18th Emma!' on it.

"I made it myself," Tanner says proudly when I notice it. The cramped unplanned spacing is just one of the imperfections that makes it much more special. There's nothing else like it.

Once I take it all in, Bennett spins me around and kisses me.

"Stop hogging her!" Diane calls out from the chorus of shouts and whistles. Davis, Andre, Justin, and others from town that I know make up the crowd. I recognize each face. I have no doubts they're here for me. Once Bennett frees me, Diane sweeps me into a hug.

These people have so seamlessly woven me into their lives. When I dream of the future, I've started inserting them in more and more pieces. I think of Christmases with homemade ornaments instead of color-coordinated themes. The Sorensons have quickly become more than summer people, adding refreshing brightness to my life. Whenever I go back home, I can't help but think that Harriettesville is the real world. When I'm with my parents, I'm just playing pretend, counting down the days until I can be myself again.

It doesn't take long before Diane breaks out bottles of white wine, insisting that if I can legally drink in Europe, then I can drink at her house.

When it's time for gifts, Diane hands me a jewelry box that holds starfish earrings encrusted with delicate gemstones. Bennett's present is a Portland College hoodie. I still have a few months before decisions come out, but I'm staying optimistic.

We escape sometime past midnight with a bottle of cheap champagne. He holds my hand the entire way back to my house.

When we enter the living room, there are strings of lights emitting a soft glow. Heaps of pillows and blankets are layered in front of the TV. The house looks closer to what I always hoped it would, inviting and warm.

"When did you do this?" I had been here just a couple of hours before.

"I enlisted help. Tanner might have a career as an interior decorator." He pops the bottle open and pours it into two plastic cups.

"With this and his signs, he definitely has a bright future," I giggle, taking a sip, already a bit tipsy from the wine at the party.

"Let's not talk about my brother anymore." He takes the cup from my hand and places it on the table before guiding me down to the nest of blankets. I don't remember the movie. I'm so lost in his touch. There is nothing else worth noticing.

For the first time, I wake up next to Bennett. His arms are draped around me, and as I shift, he pulls me closer. The sun has just started to rise, light breaking through the backdoor windows.

"I can't wait to do this every day next year." I nuzzle closer to him.

"That's the only bad part of college. Knowing that I have to wait one more semester for it to be absolutely perfect." He continues, "You'll love Maine. What if I drive through D.C. on the way up next summer to pick you up, and we'll hit up some of the national parks nearby? I've gotten really into hiking, and I want to share that with you. I know you'll love it."

"I can't think of anything better." I want that so bad. The excitement in his voice as he paints this part of our future is infectious. These dreams are so close to being real. "I think I'll love you forever. For the rest of my summers."

"Promise?" he asks.

In response, I hold out my pinkie, and he takes it in his own.

We draw out our morning together. I'm making pancakes wearing the Portland College hoodie he gave me last night. The dough is a bit lumpy, but I get them golden brown.

Later, as I'm climbing out of the shower, my phone is ringing. Wrapped in a towel, I look down to find Corrina's contact on the screen. She had sent the customary 'Happy Birthday' text yesterday, so there is no reason she should be calling. Something has to be wrong.

"Hey, Corrina."

"They're selling the summer house," she announces, jumping right in. There is no need for pleasantries when she's trying to get something done.

"Why?" I didn't see any real reason. My parents' financial situation is far more than comfortable, and Mom had been more excited than usual last summer. Is it because I'm about to go to college?

"Mom was cheating on Dad with some townie all summer. He figured it out and immediately listed the house. They already have a buyer."

"They're getting a divorce." It's not a question. It's what people do in these situations.

"Honestly, I don't think they will. This isn't the first time this has happened. Why do you think we have the summer house in the first place? Dad isn't the best at giving gracious gifts unless he wants something."

"What the hell do you mean?" How could they not get a divorce? It has always been obvious they don't love each other. I can count on one hand the number of times I'd seen them kiss when we were kids. There's no reason for them to stay together. This should be the reason to finally split.

"I swear they've been having affairs their whole marriage. The only reason they stopped was that they wanted to be good parents when you were growing up. That didn't last long, though. They just got better at hiding and burying it under gifts and parties. Come on, Emma. This is a fucked up cycle they'll never break." She laughs, but it sounds empty. "It's time you take a second to look around. It's never been hard to see. It's your own fault you didn't notice."

"Ok." The world beneath me tilts. I grip the wall because I have forgotten how to stand. It is my fault. I was here the entire summer and was so wrapped up in my own happiness I didn't see what was happening.

"I just wanted to tell you. I know you're there now, and I felt like it would be wrong if you didn't know this could be the last time. Call me if you need."

"Ok," I repeat. It's the only word I can summon.

She hangs up.

My stone cold sister, who takes on the world, had carried this by herself. They hadn't been great parents to either of us, just people who occupied the same house as us and funded us as long as our achievements met their standards. They didn't try for either of us, but at least they put on a facade for me. They never gave her the luxury of pretending they were in love.

It makes sense when I let myself think about it. We had been happy for a while. I think back on the memories before I was seven, and they whir around my head like a fever dream. My mother and father laughing with each other. Corrina smiling with no ulterior motive. The fragments are so out of character, so normal, that they feel outlandish when they drift into focus.

There are two events that I hadn't connected to until now. My mother visited her sister in Spain for a month, and the sadness that hovered over her whenever she was in a room with my father for a year after.

Corrina was fourteen. But that's when she was supposed to be having messy first loves and heartbreaks; instead, she was given something impossible to carry alone.

When I was fourteen, I came here for the first time. I hadn't learned about love from my parents. I learned it from Diane and Richard. Now, I'm learning it from Bennett.

It hits me in waves, and all I can do is stare off into the horizon through the window. There had never been any book clubs or day trips to the spa.

This will be my last time here.

My family is falling apart, and all I can think about is the summer house. I've been so willfully ignorant of it even before the summer house. Like Corrina said, it's my fault for not noticing.

When I feel able to move, I tug on clothes and run to the Sorenson house. I can't be alone. I find Bennett outside, and I rush into his arms.

"My mom was cheating on my dad with someone here all summer. He figured it out, and they're selling the house."

I'm struggling to breathe as the words rush out. "I don't want to leave. I can't picture a summer not being here with you, Diane, and the beach."

"Hey, you can always stay with us. There is always room for you here." He rubs my back in slow circles. I sob until his t-shirt is soaked with my tears. He gets up to grab me water.

In his absence, my mind starts running faster in every possible direction. Maybe it's the paranoia of the moment that leads me to the thought, but why isn't he shocked? Why isn't he asking more questions? Bennett usually wants to know every detail about something, but he is so quiet.

"Bennett, why aren't you more surprised?" I ask when he returns with a glass of water.

He looks like he's trying to compose himself, to pick the right words before telling me another part of this hellish story.

"I'm sorry. I wanted to tell you. It's just..." He struggles because there are no right words. Nothing he can say would make it ok. "I was going to tell you tonight."

"How long have you known?" My voice runs cold.

"Since June. You were so excited about how much better she was; I didn't want to ruin that. Then you left, and it felt wrong to tell you over the phone. I wanted to tell you in person. I'm so sorry." Six months. He had known for six months. The entire time we've been together, he's kept this from me. He had told me he loved me, and he still betrayed me.

"You didn't think I could handle it? This is my life. You don't get to choose what I can handle! What happens when something happens at college? We can't just stay in this perfect little bubble forever. I know I love to escape and pretend everything is perfect, but that's my choice to make." My voice rises, and the tightness in my chest starts to burn.

"It's like when you didn't say something about Jones and your sister. There just wasn't a good time."

"This is nothing like that." I want to shove him for even making the comparison. Things were so different then; we were younger and hadn't made so many promises. "My family is absolutely fucked up, and you're comparing that to a hookup that our siblings had years ago." I want to scream at him about having his perfect family. He doesn't understand because he never doubts that they all love each other. I had just been given hope that things were about to get better. Instead, they're only worse. I want to throw all this in his face, but that isn't fair.

"What about the fact that you never said anything about my brother almost kissing you? How long were you planning on hanging on to that?" Bennetts demands. That moment with Tanner had disappeared from my mind so long ago.

"Nothing happened between us. I never saw him that way."

"Then why did you hide it if there wasn't anything to feel guilty about? Do you know what he said? Right after you left last summer, he looked at me and said, 'At least she let one of us kiss her.' I've never wanted to hurt someone so badly before. He thought you had already told me and that I was fine with it. Do you want to know why he thought that? Because we tell each other everything."

"I didn't want to hurt you. I thought it would fuck everything up."

"That's exactly what I'm saying right now. Why is it enough when you do it but not for me!"

"If you can't tell the difference between the two situations, maybe we shouldn't be talking right now."

I tear away from him. He tries to hold on to my hand, but I won't let him. When he follows me saying things, my brain refuses to process them.

"Don't run away from this. You just said it. You escape from things. Will you run away next time we fight too? How are we supposed to make this work in college if you can't handle it here?" He's never spoken to me like this before. I flinch at the truth in his words. This isn't the real world. Our perfect little bubble finally pops.

"Maybe we aren't supposed to work in the real world," I say what we've been dancing around.

"You don't mean that." The anger on his face shifts to horror. I don't want to mean it, but this hurts too much for it not to be true.

"I need to be by myself." It's a lie. I ran to him, hoping he could hold all my pieces together until the storm passed. But if I stay, I won't be able to take back the words swimming in my mind.

I don't turn the lights on when I get inside. I sit in the middle of our dark, empty house. There is a skeleton of the setup Bennett made last night. Instead of being warm and cheery, it's one more reminder that things won't ever be simple. He had sat here with me, promising he loved me, but this entire time he was keeping something so important from me. This place was never destined to be a home. I don't turn on the lights before settling onto the couch, I don't trust my legs to make it up the stairs.

I wake up shivering. I had forgotten to turn up the heat last night and only grabbed a throw before I fell asleep. My phone must have fallen to the floor in the night. I pick it up to find ten texts from Bennett and a voicemail from Tanner. They all boiled down to that he was sorry and would give me space if I need it, but he wanted to know that I was ok. Tanner was checking in too. How many people knew? Was I so absorbed in Bennett last summer that I was the last to see it?

There's no way I can drive home, so I just sit. There is cereal in the cabinet but no milk, so I just eat it out of the box. The silence becomes suffocating, so I turn on the TV.

Once I find the energy to pack, I'm in the car. I don't remember the drive. Cammie was on the phone with me the entire time, making sure I could manage it by myself. I'm not sure what we talked about.

My mother is in the front room when I get in.

"Emma, why are you home early?"

"I think Bennett and I broke up."

"I'm happy that you're finally coming to your senses. We have dinner with the Fosters at eight. I hope you can join now that you're back early."

I hadn't come crawling to her in need of comfort, but this isn't the way mothers are supposed to react to their daughter's first breakup. Her words sting like a slap to the face. Mothers are supposed to offer ice cream or hugs, not a disinterested glance and a stuffy dinner. More than anything, I needed her to tell me that maybe it was only a fight or misunderstanding, but her words only solidified my fears.

My relationship with Bennett was a phase doomed from the start. Once we saw each other outside the rose-colored glasses of sunlit beaches and lazy days, we immediately snapped into two.

She doesn't mention selling the house or any of what Corrina said. I don't try to bring it up. I don't have any fight left in me right now.

I would have thought this was any other day if I didn't know. The stagnant normalcy of the house makes me feel trapped. I'm the only one seeing the big picture for the first time, and it is driving me crazy. How can they all just act like nothing happened? That selling the beach house is some instant cure for everything wrong with the situation.

I'm in my room trying to convince myself to unpack my bag. I had planned to stay for an entire weekend. I would have to look at the unworn clothes and think about what I could have been doing at the beach instead. That's how Corrina finds me, sitting on the floor next to my full duffle.

"You're only there a couple of months a year. What do you even know about this guy?" Corrina asks. She must have overheard when I came in earlier.

I know the taste of his lips fresh out of the ocean, salty and sweet. I know that he hates decaf coffee and loves strawberry ice cream. I know that his lip quirks up when he's waiting to say something but is still listening. I don't say any of this.

I also don't say four summers add up to a year's worth of days. That in between those months, there were endless texts and calls.

I can't open my mouth to fight this battle in his defense.

I just cry.

I have been crying a lot these last few days, and the tears feel like a cheap default for releasing my emotions.

The next morning, I find a toasted bagel by my bed.

Corrina and I find some understanding in the six days before she goes back to Boston. For a brief time, she's the glue that holds me together. I used to say I'd rather have no sister than deal with her, but this truce makes me see the small ways she shows up. She had somehow learned how to love from our parents, and I can't fault her for that.

My father still hasn't returned to the house.

It's snowing, thick white flakes falling that make me feel locked into this place. I take my fresh cup of coffee and head back upstairs. When I take a sip, the liquid scorches my tongue, but I ignore it.

Walking down the hall, I find my mother crying in her room. The door is cracked open, so I can see her shaking shoulders. The sobs wracking her form are silent. It's a hidden, practiced type of sadness that can only be performed in private. For the first time in my life, I feel sorry for her.

Did she love that man? Does knowing she can't go back to the same type of torture for her as it is for me? Seeing her happy during those months and then watching her shut off again in the city was upsetting. I had just thought it was the magic of the beach and that she would be full of light again next year.

There is no next year.

They don't fight when my father eventually comes back. They don't glance up when the other enters a room. I can't help but feel that I am the only living thing here.

Watching them keep up the charade creates a fissure in me, letting out the anger I've been suppressing.

We're getting ready for a dinner when it becomes too much. Watching her adjust a necklace in preparation to stand next to my father all night long makes my fragile control snap.

"Why do you stay with Dad?" I know it's the question lurking at the back of all of our minds. There is nothing in this family that's worth preserving by forcing us all under one roof. It's not the money; she has plenty of it on her own.

"What are you talking about?" Her placid smile shifts almost imperceptibly, but I see it in the mirror.

"Why do you stay with him when you don't love him? You both just sleep with other people while we all live in the same house."

"It's not that simple." She turns to me.

"Did you ever even love each other?"

"Love isn't like that. It doesn't stick around when you need it to," she says. In this moment, I believe they were in love, even for a fleeting time.

"So, you both just gave up?"

"He struck the first blow, and I got caught up managing the wreckage."

"That's not a good enough excuse."

"It's not an excuse; it's just what happened. We live with it."

"You don't have to, though."

Her mask is firmly back in place, unwavering. She makes one final adjustment to the straps of her dress. She looks perfect. "Your father is waiting. We don't want to embarrass him by being late."

The physical distance of being home makes fixing things feel out of reach. Neither of us reaches out for days. It's a battle of who will hold on to their pride the longest, and I win. I delete the texts as soon as I get the notifications.

At some point, I decline my offer of admission to Portland when I get the email and choose Haven instead. My parents are happy when I decide to choose a university nearby. I don't tell anyone it's the first other offer I found in my email. I just needed to know where I was going next.

Ignoring Bennett's texts eventually becomes a habit as strong as talking to him had been.

I go to prom with the wrong guy because anyone is wrong except for him. It doesn't matter that Michael is nice and gave the perfect proposal. He held up an honest to God boombox in the middle of the courtyard and a sign that said, *"Say Yes to Prom With Me Emma."*

Cammie and I made an entire day of dress shopping. After I had told her everything that happened between Bennett and me, she's made a point of going out to do things with me. My dress is made of sleek satin and made me feel like an old Hollywood star when I first tried it on.

Now, I realize I had picked the dress with a different version of the night in mind. It's the dress that fits my desperate delusion that Bennett will show up and follow through on all the plans we made. He'll have figured out the color of my dress and come in a matching tux. It's the dress I picture when I think about him dancing with me.

But that half-hearted dream dies as I take Michael's hand and climb into the limo.

Michael kisses me at the after-prom. I try to kiss him back but end up running away to find a shot of vodka that eventually becomes three. It's the first night I ever get really, truly drunk. I end the night back at home, curled up on my bathroom floor. Someone must have driven, but I don't remember who.

I texted Bennett at some point in the night. Telling him I missed him. He never responds. It's a brutal punctuation of what was supposed to be a night of us dancing next to a fake backdrop of the Eiffel Tower.

When I get to school on Monday, Cammie tells me Michael hooked up with a girl named Harper Cross. Cammie's insistent that it's the biggest deal ever that he ditched me, but I don't care. At least one of us had a good senior prom.

The rush of final exams gives me a distraction. It's the most I've ever studied, even though they're only formalities for seniors.

Graduation is fine. Our Valedictorian faints mid-speech, which is more entertaining than his thoughts about us 'chasing new horizons.' Corrina couldn't make it, but my parents are in the stands. They don't cheer, just clap politely as I cross the stage. We're all here only because we're supposed to. If it wasn't for Cammie, I don't think I would have walked for graduation at all.

The day marks another rite of passage that is not quite right. Each step has giant Sorenson shape holes.

14

Summer

Four years ago

I had clung to a perpetual string of 'next summer,' assuming a forever. I thought the beach house would settle into the unchanging pattern of my life. But those summers in Harriettesville were separate from the other parts of my life. It was foolish to think that they would follow the same rules.

Now, as June first comes and goes, I'm not at the beach. I am certain I will never have a summer with him again. My body is wound tight with anticipation to feel the ocean air, free of traffic-filled streets and the never-ending need to be moving.

It's an exercise in restraint to stop my mind from wandering on its own while my body stays rooted in reality. The solution is easy: let go. But I don't think I'll ever be able to leave our summers behind.

I float through the events my parents are invited to, but I'm never really present. It's a look into what summers might have been if I had never left. Now that I know the difference, the city is dull in comparison. If we had never gotten the beach house, there's a chance I could be happy dressing up and sneaking champagne.

I'm surrounded by faces that I have known since cotilion, ones that belong to future boardroom executives and politicians. Maybe, in another life, I'd have run off to clubs with them and would have made different types of mistakes.

As I pack the final set of boxes for my move to Haven University, my mother makes another passing comment about how now I'm ready for a real boyfriend.

She acts like Bennett was a set of training wheels I can throw away as I enter the real world. I'm unsure if I can have another relationship at all, 'real' or otherwise. I can't put myself in a place to be hurt again or even want someone enough that they could hurt me.

It's during the first week of classes that Cammie mentions therapy. She's been there for late night phone calls and crying over sappy movies during my breakup. There has been enough of her for me, but I can't muster the energy to be there for her.

"Didn't you see it coming, though? You're in France, and she's in Florida," I respond to her, telling me that she and Vanessa, the girl she went to prom with, broke up.

"What the hell, Emma?" The sharpness and shock in her voice wrenches my focus away from cleaning the dirt out from under my nails.

"What?"

"I've been there through all your shit these past few months, and you can't even pretend to care about what's going on in my life. I knew it was going to end, but that doesn't make it hurt any less. I just needed my best friend to tell me that I'm right, and it sucks. That it's her loss, and I'll find some hot French girl to drink wine with. I want to keep being there for you, But I'm not sure if I can if you're not willing to figure your stuff out. Please talk to someone," her soft tone cuts deep, driving home the truth in what she's saying.

"I'm sorry."

"It's ok. I just need you. I miss you."

I'm not sure if I finally call Dr. Holmes because I feel like I need help or if I'm just scared of losing Cammie. During our first session, I'm not sure where to start. Am I here because of my family or because of a boy? I feel embarrassed admitting the second possibility, so I don't until a few months in.

When I do talk about Bennett and the Sorensons, I realize it wasn't one or the other. My love for the Sorensons was the opposite of what I had at home. It's what I might still have if I didn't push them away.

Going to therapy helps, but I'm still disconnected. When I start freshman year, I'm a shadow of myself. Even though I have no interest in my classes, the routine gives me something to rely on. On the worst days, I can shut myself off and let my body carry me where I need to go.

I try to stay in contact with Cammie, but she is in Paris for school. The time zones make it impossible to call. We make it work for the first few months, but once classes pick up, we are stuck texting with an occasional drunk video call while the other is eating lunch.

When she talks about her new friends, I don't want to resent that she's found people so easily. She'll always find a place to fit wherever she goes. I've only felt that way with two people for me over the last eighteen years. One of them is countries away, and the other I can't bear to talk to anymore.

Cammie is determined to help me, "You just have to go to some events. Say yes to the parties you say your roommate is trying to drag you to."

"I guess."

"You are so damn lovable, and I get to say that as a certified people hater. But you are purposely blocking that part of yourself right now."

I start to go out more with Beth. Eventually, I'm saying yes to every pregame and event.

I meet guys at these parties.

Guys, that feel like a cure. Sometimes in the dim lights, I imagine they have dark, sandy hair and a faded scar. I can pretend this is all a dream. Each night I am free, but in the morning, when the hangover hits, I roll over to see a face I can only vaguely remember from the night; before the effect has faded.

THE SUMMERS WE LEFT BEHIND

I discovered that losing yourself in others is easier than accepting your own thoughts.

That's how I find myself with no blanket on a twin sized bed this morning. I'm not sure how late it is, but light is already piercing through the gaps in the blinds. Because I don't have to untangle myself from the sheets, I nearly have a clean getaway. Just as I make it to the door, I catch his sleep heavy eyes fixed on me.

"Bye, John. I'll text you," I say, having no intention of seeing him again. He had seemed interesting at the band party last night, talking about how the film industry is going downhill but how he went to an indie film festival last fall that gave him hope for the next generation.

It turned out that all John knows about, or thinks about, are movies and knowing more about movies than anyone else. While taking off my shirt, he explained the difference between a film and a movie, which I promptly tuned out.

"Actually, it's Jake," he says. In the daylight, I see that his side of the dorm is splattered with signed movie posters. I didn't pick it out last night, but his bedspread has the Pulp Fiction logo scattered all over it. *Did I really just fuck someone with a Tarantino shrine?*

"Oh, bye, Jake," I say again. I'm not as embarrassed as I should be as I slip out of his dorm. It's not the first time it's happened.

"I'm finally seeing other people," I tell Cammie days later as I scrub off my eyeliner and get ready for sleep. It's one in the morning here. One of the biggest benefits of staying out late is that I get to call Cammie as she starts her day.

"Who? I need a name, how you met, even a social security number if you have it." I can hear a kettle whistling on her end. She's gotten really into alternative teas at school.

"I mean, there's a few. Just guys I've met at parties and stuff. Nothing serious." I wince, realizing she thought I was actually *dating* someone new.

"Hell, yeah. You were emotionally dating him for like four years. Get him out of your system. Just get tested. College guys are nasty." She's good about never saying his name. I never asked her to, but it helps.

We chat more about classes and how she might not be back for the summer because she has an offer to be in a junior curators program in Greece. I want to be more excited for her, but she was the only reason I survived being in the city last year. We are going in different directions. I'm stuck in the same place while she is becoming everything she was born to be.

At the end of the year, Beth lets me know she's living with some of the girls she's met on the soccer team next year. I had been putting off housing plans for months, hoping I would find someone.

Beth moves out a day earlier than me. I watch her take the last stack of boxes and shut the door behind her.

I'm alone.

I'm back where I started at the beginning of the year. Actually, this is worse. Everyone has settled into a routine with their new friends and people they plan on spending the next three years with, but I'm still just floating.

15
Friday
Now

I sneak back into the house. My body has gone numb from drinking in nostalgia under the night sky.

I had thought that at least Libby or Caleb would have been awake for the meteor shower. It's three in the morning, and everyone is silent despite insisting that they would wake up in time. I slip into the fridge and grab some iced coffee. Hot is preferable, but I don't want to wake anyone up.

Secretly, I want to do this alone.

I sip my coffee, watching the expanse of the sky.

Footsteps come up behind me, swishing against the sand. I know it's him before he says anything. There is something terribly wrong and hardwired in me that knows when he's close.

"I guess we're the only ones that made it," he says as he sits down next to me in the sand.

"I guess we are," I nod. So, we're not going to talk about last night.

A meteor races across the sky, giving purpose to our silence. Each a shooting star. If wishes were guaranteed to come true, would I ask to go back in time? Would I tell my fourteen-year-old self to unpack her bags before going to the beach? But that would just delay the inevitable. Even if I didn't meet Bennett that first night it would have been at Books or Early Bird or the beach on a different night.

The moment I stepped foot in Harriettesville, we were destined to become us.

Before too long, the sun starts to crest the horizon, breaking the spell.

"This feels too damn familiar," I let loose a sigh.

"I have a question for you."

"Ok?"

"Do I get to break your pinkie?" He's referring to the last promise we ever made to one another. I might have thought he was serious if he had asked this a week ago. Now, I know it's something else.

"Will you regret knowing the answer?"

"Only if it's yes." His eyes bore into me. *Is he asking if I still love him? Right here?*

"Will I regret asking you the same question?"

"What answer do you want from me?"

"The honest one." After last night I need to know too.

"You and I both know being honest has never been our strong suit."

"Then let's at least be honest right now."

"You first." He gingerly holds my hand, playfully squeezing the finger in question.

"No. You?"

"No, never. It was a promise too hard to break even if I had really tried."

I break away from his touch, "Can you just tell me what you want? I can't figure you out anymore, and I don't want to spend the last few days here trying to solve you like some fucked up puzzle. I keep wanting to stop wanting you, but I can't. Give me a reason now, and I'll walk away. Say the word, and I won't ever come within a hundred miles of this place or Chicago again."

"Stay." That single word makes me want to cry. There is so much weight behind what he means, but it's not enough.

"Then what are we? Friends again?" I hope he'll say yes, to give me that much of him back.

In answer, he seals his lips to mine. Telling me the words he longs to convey just by pressing into me. His touch is soft and searching.

I gasp.

It's enough. He had always been enough, but had I?

He begins to break away, taking my surprise as a refusal. I cup the back of his head and pull him back to me. The second kiss isn't tender. Our lips clash with the force of every argument we never had, reclaiming what others had touched. My hand runs up his jaw feeling the light graze of stubble before I thread my fingers through his hair. He guides me to the ground until my back is pressed against the sand and his hand is gripping my thigh.

"I could never go back to being just friends after knowing what it's like to love you. I couldn't stand not touching you or knowing you love someone else. Will you come back to me? We can forget all the summers in between and just be us again." There was nothing I wanted more.

Yes, begins forming on my lips, but I'm cut off by the abrupt noise of the sliding door and the disheveled group that stumbles through it. My body feels empty without his heat on top of me.

"Sorry guys, it's over already," I say from the ground. If they just leave, I can finish this conversation that's been years in the making. When I turn to where Bennett was standing, he's already gone heading back to his house. The high I had been riding from our kiss starts to fade. Now that I have him back, I don't want him to go.

I look down at my phone as it lights up, and though there is no contact for the number, I know it's his. I had memorized it the first time he had given it to me.

Bennett: Later.

My heart skips at the promise of more of him.

"Well, at least we can watch the sunrise," Caleb says.

"Looks like someone had a roll in the sand," Jess grins, looking in the direction of the Pink House.

We soak in the scene until someone's stomach audibly rumbles.

I keep replaying what happened on the beach for the rest of the morning, trying to convince myself it isn't a hallucination brought on by the cosmic event.

"So, did you two finally attempt to strangle each other, or did you kiss and make up? Both?" Jess asks.

"Why would we do either of those things?" I say as I gather hot dog supplies from the kitchen.

"Oh, the tension. The glares. Or maybe the history of long lost love. Who knows, maybe I'm just speculating." I must make a face. Actually, I know I make a face because up until this point, I thought we hid it so well. "You're kidding. We've spent the entire week on the sidelines letting it play out."

"Sorry."

"What is there to be sorry for? You gave us some quality entertainment."

"I've been moping around this week. First, with Jackson, and then figuring stuff out with Bennett. None of you signed up for that when you let me tag along," I say.

"We signed up for all of it the moment we became your friends. Break ups happen, so do messy run-ins with exes. It will take a lot more to get rid of us."

"I've been so absent, and you guys still brought me."

"To be honest, it feels like it's been a while since we've seen you. We love every version of you, but it was weird missing someone that was standing next to you. Whenever we were with you and Jackson, it was like whenever your parents visited. You just tucked yourself away. I always thought it was weird to see that side of you when we knew the other parts of you. Remember when you insisted on joining a hot chili eating contest? After meeting your family, I had no idea where that side of you came from. Meeting him and seeing you two together, it all makes sense now." She sighs, "So, no, I don't think any of us are upset. We're just happy to have you back."

She's right. When I'm with Bennett, I'm me again.

As I'm putting ketchup on my hot dog, my phone rings on the table.

"You can just turn it off," I yell to Libby as she picks it up.

"Actually, you might want to take this. It's Jackson. I think it's time to tell him to go to hell." She holds up the screen to show me as the ketchup misses my plate entirely and splatters on my shirt.

Shit. I snatch the phone and head upstairs to change.

"Hey, babe. Your mom called, and I just really need to explain everything," he says when I pick up.

"Now you need to talk? Did you lose your phone for a week?"

"I had been meaning to tell you that I wanted to end things, but we were both so busy with the trip and graduation. Then Shelby was just there, and if we weren't going to be together much longer anyways…"

"Let me make sure I'm clear on what you're saying. You are calling me to explain why you cheated on me instead of just breaking up with me because *my mom* asked you to? Do you not hear how absolutely fucked up that logic is? Were you going to wait until we moved to the same city to live together? Fuck you, Jackson. I hope you're enjoying the bacteria infested hot tub without me." I hang up.

I wish I had a flip phone to slap it shut and cut off the call. Still, pressing the button to hang up is liberating in a way I didn't know I needed. I had spent days thinking about how little our relationship had actually meant, and he finally gave me the opportunity to officially say goodbye.

I had never been scared of Jackson leaving. I never held on to him like he was something precious, our love something to be treasured. I told him I loved him. I loved him like you love your neighbor's dog, convenient affection. I was never in love with him. I know that now. I just said it enough that I had myself convinced. That first night of drunken mourning was more in memory of the time I had invested in curating the perfect relationship.

Jackson was the right person for a version of me that never had the chance to exist. The version of the girl that never came to the beach. No, he's the wrong person that a different version of me would have settled for.

I peel off my top and run it under cold water. The stain is probably a lost cause, but hey, at least I'm trying. I grab one of the remaining clean tops from my bag and throw it on.

"What did he want?" Jess asks. I can see everyone's ears perk up around the table.

"He didn't want to hurt me by breaking up, so he needed to fuck someone else to get it out of his system. Or some shit like that," I say.

"Make that make sense," Amber rolls her eyes.

"That's what I said. But his number is blocked and deleted." Everyone at the table applauds, and I take a bow.

After dinner, we make our way to the beach, hauling wood and blankets.

I've never set up a bonfire before. I had only attended a few, and the fire was always already in progress, ready to be enjoyed. Even when we went camping, I sat back and watched the process. It turns out there's a lot more involved than just lighting a match and tossing in on some wood.

Caleb, our resident pyromaniac, takes the lead, creating a ring of rocks. The rest of us are handing him little branches and logs for him to arrange just so.

We've finally built what Caleb considers a passable structure as the sun dips below the horizon. Still, we're not done. The match flickers and it takes multiple attempts to catch the kindling as Caleb mutters under his breath about the wind.

Bennett's group hasn't joined, but I have no doubt they got an invite. I'm buzzing at the idea of seeing him again. He hadn't given me a concrete answer this morning, but I'm still hopeful based on his initial reaction. Now that I have given myself permission to want him again, it's hard to think of anything else.

We've laid out towels and found some more substantial logs to sit on. It's nearly dark by the time they join.

"Theo, you lost," Jess shouts across the beach, playfully flipping him off.

"Does that mean she didn't strangle him?" He calls back.

"Traitors," I say as Theo slips a ten into Jess's hand.

"Sorry for taking so long, but Diane's dinner was worth savoring," Jordan explains as they settle in.

"Diane?" Amber asks. Up until this point, no one has mentioned her.

"Bennett's mom," I explain. It's weird to think they don't know something I've considered essential. I feel guilty for not taking her up on her invitation to stop by the house. I had been waiting for the tension between Bennett and me to dissipate. Now that we're in the clear, I want everyone to meet her. It's hard not to love Diane, but I want them to know her the same way I do.

Theo unpacks the s'mores supplies they brought while Jordan passes around beers. I like our little routine. My friends make the plans, and Bennett's show up with supplies. It makes sense our friends would get along.

As we all begin to settle, I can't help but notice how close Jess sits to Caleb.

"Hey." Bennett sits beside me, and I know my smile is as big as the one taking up his face. Our knees knock together, and he rests his arm behind me. I lean in until my head is resting on his shoulder. "I like that you're wearing my shirt."

I look down and see that I had grabbed the grey Portland College hoodie. It feels right to be wearing it here. It's another snapshot of what could have been, but this time I'm not left feeling empty.

Libby gives me a surprised but approving look. *You're spilling everything later.*

I gave her a look back. *Oh. My. God.* I know, right? I had only told Jess because she asked, but now that I am officially free of Jackson, I'm ready to embrace the possibility of Bennett.

Everyone else has headed back to the houses leaving Bennett and me to watch the last of the glowing embers fade. He starts to kiss down the side of my neck. I want him to keep going. But I need answers to everything that we keep leaving unresolved.

"Can we talk?" I ask.

"Why do we need to talk?" His hand starts to rub up and down my leg, challenging my concentration.

"Everything."

"I don't want to think about any of that anymore. We're back to the way things were." He looks hurt. As if my desire to talk out the past negates the present. "I have you back, and that's all that matters."

"Bennett, I'm serious. The way we used to be ended up with us not speaking for four years." Being back like this isn't enough. We're at the brink of something great we just need to get over the edge.

"Fine. You really fucking hurt me, and I broke your trust. I don't want to relive any of that. We'll do better now that we made mistakes. Does that answer your questions?"

"What do we look like outside of Harriettesville? We've never been anywhere together besides this place. We're in a completely different spot now. I'm not about to join you in law school the same way we planned for college. I don't even know what I'm planning for next year."

"Then come to Chicago. You can live with me, and we'll work it all out then."

I jerk away from him. "It's been less than a day since we agreed we want this again. I'm not moving in with you. We still haven't even been together outside of here."

"I want to be with you, and you want to be with me. Why isn't that enough?" He's pleading with me now.

"We are enough." I pull his head to my shoulder, losing my fingers in his hair. "I'm just scared of jumping into this again without a plan. I'm scared to lose you again. I don't think I could survive that a second time."

"I don't want to lose you either."

Somewhere in the silence, we understand that this is the start of unpacking what neither of us truly left behind. I still feel the weight of everything unsaid and begging to be heard. But a start is enough for now.

I want to sleep in his arms on the beach, but it's not summer. If it was summer, it would be easier to pretend we have nothing to fix. The chill keeps me in reality, preventing the fantasy from creeping in. With the fire extinguished, the cold seeps through, even with the heat of Bennett's body pressing into mine.

16
Fall

Three years ago

I didn't find my friends all at once during my sophomore year. There was no cosmic event or heroic task that thrust us all together. Libby and I have always been the most different and likely wouldn't have crossed paths if we weren't randomly assigned roommates.

When I open the door to my sophomore dorm, I find her balancing on a bedpost, attempting to put up a giant tapestry of a tarot card. She has this look of an acrobat casually staying in an uncomfortable position.

"Hey, do you have any extra Command hooks? I think I miscalculated."

"Sure," I dive into my collection of stuff and hand her what she needs before she loses her balance and topples over. "You're Libby, right? Unless I'm in the wrong room cause I've had that dream at least three times this week."

"That's me." She hops down, inspecting her work, "It looks a little crooked, doesn't it? I think I'll just leave it unless it bugs you. If it does, please tell me."

"No, I think it's great," I'm a little in awe of the space. There's no way she's been here more than an hour, and the three walls on her side of the room are already covered. Her nightstand has a pyramid of contraband candles and a stack of comic books.

"Also, don't worry about candles or anything like that. I hooked up with our RA over the summer, and she's really chill."

After that, Libby doesn't give me much choice about being her friend. Like me, she doesn't know anyone on campus. She has just transferred to Haven after leaving the track team at one of those uptight Christian universities that have a curfew and dress code. Looking at Libby, I can tell she made the right choice. Crop tops and tattoos are her uniform, and I can't picture her any other way.

My freshman year roommate invited me out or offered to pick up tampons, but Libby is more. She fills up the empty spaces in my life to the point it's impossible to mope around the same way I did before.

We pregame campus events with cheap wine. RA supervised tote painting is far more enjoyable when you don't care about the result and spend half the time laughing. We make memories.

She shares parts of her life through the little things. She teaches me her grandmother's kimchi recipe. We use her contraband hot plate and air frier whenever we want a home cooked meal.

With each smiling snapshot, I become myself again. She doesn't realize that with each invitation and genuine smile, she's pulling me out of the hole I've dug myself into.

It's a week after classes start before we meet any of the others.

"You're. Fucking. Kidding me." A Black girl with a Southern accent is pretending to punch the door in front of her. I've seen her before coming in and out of the dorm a few doors down.

"Everything ok?" I ask. I'm on the way back from doing laundry and forgot a bag to carry the clothes, so I'm struggling to keep socks and underwear from dropping on the floor.

"My roommate forgot to tell me that her long distance boyfriend is in town. I've officially been sexiled, and I really don't want to wear this anymore."

"Interview?" I guess based on the skirt suit she's wearing.

"No, presentation for a business class. Why do they feel the need to take that shit so seriously?"

"I'm just three doors over. You can hang out and change if you want. Borrowing sweatpants is practically the college equivalent of asking your neighbor for sugar.

When we reach my dorm, I try the door moving the handle with my hip, it's unlocked, so I know Libby is home. And thank God because I'm not sure how I would have gotten my keys out of my pocket with the load of clothes in my arms.

"Hey, I found a stray. Can we keep her?" I call out, giving Libby a brief warning about our company.

"Oh, you're Maggie's roommate, right? Jess?" Libby asks, looking up from her laptop.

"Yeah, but I'm not her biggest fan right now," Jess grumbles.

"Long distance boyfriend decided to visit," I explain.

"There's no way that lasts the semester. I've heard her talk about him, and I honestly think they hate each other. High school relationships almost never work out even if they last the first year," Libby says, abandoning her work at the first sound of drama.

Her words make me think about how I almost was the girl with the high school relationship. My thoughts only occasionally wander to Bennett and the Sorensons these days. Last year, our break up was the background noise to everything I did. Now he only floats back to me when someone brings up high school relationships or I drink too much cheap white wine.

Jess throws on one of my shirts and some sweats.

One of the best parts of living with Libby, besides her company, is that she has a great TV setup. After the conversation meanders to 90s movies and Jess mentions she's never seen a John Hughes movie, we set up on the ground with a bag of popcorn to watch *Ferris Bueller's Day Off*. It turns into our first sleepover.

It becomes a ritual the next time Jess gets locked out. Libby was right, Maggie's relationship only makes it one month in, but that hadn't stopped her from bringing whatever new guy she was seeing to their dorm. Before long, we've gone through John Hughes's entire filmography and moved on to 2000's romcoms.

"I don't get it. Like I am for the girls and sexual empowerment, but what's stopping her from going to their place?" Jess sighs after a particularly long day. It has gotten to the point where she keeps a toothbrush and a set of clothes in our room.

"But that would deprive us of the pleasure of your company," I say

"You are mistaken if you think you'll be able to get rid of me that easily." Jess gives us a wink. "Anyways, I want to go do something tonight. My professors have been absolute dicks this week, and I need to dance."

"There's a party off campus that some of the ceramics people are throwing. Those guys are a little pretentious, which means they always have the good beer."

When we arrive, the party is already in full swing. People are strewn about the yard, and a girl is puking in the bushes. I guess everyone got the memo about good beer.

After getting drinks, we huddle in a corner.

"I think that guy is on the football team." Jess gestures with her bottle to a huge guy next to the packed couch. It's not odd seeing athletes out with everyone else. We're not what people would consider a sports school. But she's right. The guy is something Winters, a sophomore, and part of why we're having an above average season.

It's not long before someone shouts, "Police!" Us and the rest of the underage drinkers scatter. In the frenzy, we join the group rushing through the back door. There's no gate, just a fence that everyone is scrambling over. Jess and Libby climb up with grace. When I start to scale the fence, I take my time, scared of slipping off. When I attempt to swing over to the other side, one of my legs won't move. It's not because I'm frozen in fear. Nope, my favorite jeans are caught.

I love these jeans, but they aren't worth getting arrested over. When I try to tear the fabric, they don't budge. Well, at least I know the quality is good. Jess and Libby are on the other side and haven't abandoned me. I almost tell them to leave when a voice calls out from the side of the house.

"Do you need a hand?" I look down, and the football player Jess pointed out earlier is looking up at me.

"That would be great. I really don't want to get stuck up here all night."

"Just give me one second." He climbs to the top with ease. But he fumbles with the caught fabric the same way I had.

"Tear them. I don't think they're meant to make it out of this night." At my request, I hear the rip of fabric. For the first time in my life, I am happy I wore full coverage underwear.

Once I'm free, we jump down to the other side with my friends.

"Josh." He holds out his hand. The formal introduction is odd but charming.

Turns out, he is in the dorm building next to ours, and we head back together, all swearing never to go to a ceramics party again.

The only two of my friends I meet simultaneously are Amber and Caleb in a class called 'Intro to Creative Thinking.' Like the rest of the class, I thought this was just an alternative way to say Creative Writing. The professor is a big fan of assigned group projects since it forces us to meet new people.

The projects have prompts like 'If you had all the resources in the world, how would you build an underwater railway?' or 'How would you make $50,000 with nothing more than what you can find in a craft store?' Points are given more for creativity than practicality.

We have been assigned to work together on designing our dream home with unconventional materials.

"What constitutes an unconventional material?" The girl who introduced herself as Amber asks the professor.

"Use your imagination," the professor calls back in a sing-song voice.

"I regret not dropping this class when I could have, even if it is an easy A," she says to herself. In our group introductions, she told us she's a pre-med chemistry major, which partly explains why the creative component of creative thinking is her own personal hell.

"I swear he would ask us to solve world hunger with nothing but a toothpick and a bottle of glue," Caleb says. This has Amber and me laughing.

"Or build a time machine using things you could find in a natural history museum," I add. We continue like this, bonding over the ridiculousness of the class.

After the class is dismissed for the day, we end up on the floor of my dorm, attempting to finish the project as fast as possible.

"What about a library made out of books and a game room with action figures and resin for walls," Amber says, sketching out our blueprint.

"Are books unconventional enough? They're basically just wood in a different form." Caleb is taking this part of the assignment seriously; his underwater tunnel design wasn't innovative enough, and it brought him down to a B.

"If he doesn't think it is, I will personally tell him to shove it," Amber snaps. As time passes, it becomes more apparent that our professor is her nemesis.

The door pops open, just missing Caleb, who takes up an astounding amount of space. He tries not to take up so much room, but he's so broad it can't be helped.

"I've brought provisions." Libby holds up our coffee orders. Jess and Josh follow her in. It's the first time all of us are knowingly in the same room together.

"What the hell are you doing here?" Amber shoots at Josh.

He holds up his hands in surrender, "They keep me around to carry stuff." Currently, he has both Jess's and Libby's backpacks slung over his shoulders.

"Y'all know each other?" Jess asks.

"She's that tutor I was telling you about." He had called her 'smart as shit' and 'tough as hell.' I would say that's an accurate assessment from working on the assignment with her.

After we finished for the night. We convince Caleb and Amber to come out with us.

It only takes a few months for us all to become inseparable. Amber and Josh even set aside their differences and play nice—usually.

"Amber texted that she'll be by in an hour." We are going to meet Josh and Caleb for trivia later tonight. Jess, Libby, Amber, and I were the only ones able to meet up for drinks in Libby and my dorm beforehand. Well, until Amber said something came up and that she'll be late.

Since the first time we went, the six of us have played as a team, with Josh and Amber's combined knowledge carrying us to the top three. But last week, a playful fight turned into a bet to see who between the two of them actually knows more trivia. Libby is good with art, and Jess knows random facts about history. The consensus is that Caleb and I were largely useless and only there for a good time.

The winning team gets to pick the spring break plans for next month. We are stuck between camping and a beach trip. I'm still on a beach hiatus and all for camping.

Just as I'm about to start my second tequila sour, the fire alarm goes off. So far this year, someone has set their take home exam on fire in a trash can, forgotten to take a fork out of the microwave, and sprayed perfume into a smoke detector. The fire department has become very friendly with us at this point. Jess has even gotten a couple of their numbers, 'just in case of an emergency.'

We head downstairs and make ourselves at home on the lawn. There isn't much point in going anywhere else. Because we have prime viewing, we see a couple of girls with shampoo still in their hair, and a few couples are barely dressed. We have all learned the hard way that some of the RAs check rooms to make sure people actually evacuate.

Among the barely dressed group are Josh and Amber. Jess, Libby, and I exchange looks.

"Holy shit. Y'all are seeing this too?" We don't get a chance to answer Jess because they're heading our way.

"Amber, I think you missed a button or two," Libby says, sipping the drink she's brought. Amber's eyes widen, and she fumbles with the flannel to fix the aforementioned buttons.

"Seems like trivia planning went well," Jess says. "Figure out the teams?" Amber gives a pleading look that promises we'll talk later.

We hold her to it later when ordering drinks at the bar.

"He is one of the most irritating humans I've ever met. But have you seen the guy? We also have way more in common than you'd think." I can tell she's falling for him.

To everyone's relief, Josh doesn't let her tumble into oblivion. Instead, he catches her and sweeps her away.

A month after the camping trip that Libby's team ended up choosing. I meet Jackson. We are at a party thrown by one of Caleb's fraternity brothers, and Jess and I are playing beer pong.

Isn't that the way all great love stories start?

I overshoot in a way that I would have felt embarrassed about, except that we're winning, and I'm already a few drinks in.

I start to bend down to scramble for it, but a hand snatches it from the ground and presents it to me.

"A lady should never be left to chase after her own balls." The hand is attached to a guy with an expensive smile and flashing blue eyes.

"What about someone else's balls?" I'm feeling bold tonight. I haven't hooked up with someone since before break and am desperate to break my dry spell.

He lets loose a rumbling laugh, "You can chase after mine any day."

I look for him after we win the game. A cowboy looking guy steps in to take my place, and Jess is more than pleased with her new partner.

I'm intrigued by the chase. There wasn't a spark between us exactly, but something more than the passive attraction I've had with other guys.

He's outside chatting with someone I vaguely recognize from other times we've been at the house. He ends the conversation and heads my way.

"You found me," he says.

"You gave me a challenge. What's my prize?" I'm more direct than usual, but I like this game. It reminds me of someone else.

"What do you want it to be?"

"Your name or a kiss or both."

"Jackson," he murmurs, closing the space between us. When we finally break for air, I'm on his lap in an Adirondack chair.

"I know I didn't win anything, but can I get your name and maybe your number? I really want to do more than kiss you right now, but I want to take you to dinner first," he says, pulling away. I'm not exactly getting rejected, but this isn't the way I had hoped the night would end. Still, the idea of having to continue the game we'd started was enticing.

"Emma." I give him my phone to put his number in. I want to be in control of the next move. We spend the rest of the night making out, leaving my lips so thoroughly bruised that I can still feel him when I decide to take a chance and text him the next day.

I see him more and more frequently. By the end of the first month together, we're official. I've never posted a picture of a guy besides Bennett. Even after our breakup, I still left one of the disposable pictures up. After two months, I finally post Jackson, a silly candid moment of us at dinner together. My heart sinks when I check later and see that Diane liked it.

He meets my parents during move out that year.

"I'm happy you've finally settled into your first real relationship," my mother says when we reach the car. There's that word again, real. It crawls beneath my skin. That acknowledgment, more than the pleasantries and laughs exchanged, signifies their approval.

During his summer visits, I'm closer to my family than I've ever been before.

Jackson is from Long Island and bonds with Corrina over life in New York, where she moved to after law school graduation. He helps me fit into my family, holding my hand while understanding their motivations.

I can see how we might have this life forever. Not growing something new of our own but fitting into this preset pattern.

17

Winter

One year ago

We've been together nine months by the time my 21st birthday comes around. Jackson takes me to the nicest restaurant within a reasonable distance near Haven, La Lune. It's French with small plates and big glasses of wine.

My dress makes me feel more adult than I am, black with a high neckline. I feel too formal. Amber and Jess had suggested a themed bar hopping night. If I had taken them up on it, I'd be in jeans and a coat, not four inch heels. I remind myself that one of the things I like about Jackson is that when I'm with him, I don't feel like I'm in a college relationship. Yes, we go to parties and drink cheap beer, but even then, we feel so stable.

I had always imagined my first legal drink would be a cheap shot or a can of something shitty from the gas station. Instead, it's from a three hundred dollar bottle of Cabernet. I don't even really like red wine. It makes my tongue feel heavy and always stains my lips. But it's winter, and the waiter said it pairs well with our food. The waiter doesn't

ID us when he takes our orders. I don't get to whip out my new, and very real, ID.

"I wanted to give you your gift before the appetizers come out." He pulls out a Tiffany blue bag. "Open it."

"Oh, it's beautiful." It's a gold necklace with a delicate pearl pendant. I'm impressed he picked something so elegant. I haven't worn a necklace consistently in years, but this makes me think about changing my mind.

He gets out of his chair and lifts the necklace to help me put it on. My hair's up in a loose bun, but there are still a few stray curls he has to brush out of the way. Jackson's touch is soft and mundane. Mundane in the same way as a good cup of coffee. It's reliable and adds a bit of comfort to your life.

Once he's back sitting, Jackson reaches across the table to grab my hand.

"I love you," He says.

"Love you too."

He had said it first, a week after we moved in for the Junior year. I'm not certain when I said it back. It just came one day.

I've convinced myself there are different types of love. The love I had for Bennett was only for the summers, bright and explosive. What I feel for Jackson is for every season, softer and stagnant at times.

I doubt this reasoning sometimes when I see Amber and Josh. They stay completely consumed by each other even after a year.

In those moments, I remind myself that choosing the safe route in life is underrated. You get to the place you want to go with far less pain.

He pays the bill, and we're off to the surprise party that Jess let slip a couple of weeks ago when she asked if any of his single hot friends would be there. To her credit, Jackson didn't explain to the people invited that it was supposed to be a surprise.

"I have a surprise for you." We pull up to Zenith, an old church turned cocktail bar and event space. I nearly roll my eyes. If I hadn't already known there's a surprise party waiting for me, I'd have figured it out just then.

He helps me out of the car, making sure my heels don't cause me to tumble on the bits of ice covering the sidewalk.

The room is full of people. Many of them probably came back a few days early from break just to be here. Of the crowd, I only know about seventy percent. The people I know are made up of my friends and the group of people I've met at the parties that I go to with Jackson. The others are people who obviously know Jackson by how they whoop his name when we come in and those that just tagged along with their friends.

It's perfect. Too perfect. Everything had been bought and planned so meticulously. I can see my parents' touches in the little extravagant parts like the real glassware.

"What do you think, babe?" Jackson's arm is around my waist.

"I love it," I say instead of the truth. It is always easy to lie to Jackson about my emotions. Each time he rewards me with a look of pure happiness. He makes me feel like loving someone is about keeping them happy as long as possible. Though he sometimes misses the mark, he tries.

The truth is that this all reminds me of the last time a boy gave me a birthday party. It was messy and imperfect in all the right ways. The string lights here are too well placed. The sign is professionally printed and not handmade.

Jackson pulls me onto the dance floor. I wish I had remembered a change of shoes. I can feel a blister forming on my heel already.

With each drink, I try to forget the differences. I try to forget my guilt for not being head over heels for the night my boyfriend planned. This is perfect. This is what stable people in relationships do for each other when they're in love.

But I'd never told Jackson I was in love with him, just that I loved him. To me, those things are worlds apart.

I can't help thinking *he* should be here. Why isn't he here?

I think I say those words to Jess and Libby when they find me crying in the bathroom.

"We can go get Jackson," one of them says. But I don't want that

"No. Not him," I blubber, words catching in my sobs.

I can't form the words to explain what I do want. I want Bennett. More specifically, I want it to be summer and to be sixteen again. I haven't mentioned Harriettesville or the Sorensons to anyone since I got here except my therapist. I need to keep these chapters of my life separate. I'm so dangerously close to saying his name.

"Ok. Well, I am going to tell him it's time for you to go home."

I get half carried out the back into a car.

"Who were you talking about back there?" Libby says from the driver's seat.

Jess is rubbing my back, updating me on how close we are to the apartment.

"Someone I need to forget." Someone that might haunt me forever.

The next day, my hangover is my punishment for thinking of another man all night at the party my boyfriend and parents carefully orchestrated. This is only emphasized by the sun blaring the crack in the curtains.

Libby walks in with painkillers and ginger ale in hand. "You good? You were pretty upset coming home last night."

"I'm fine. I just had too many drinks. We had a red with dinner, and I don't think that ever is a good idea," I say.

"Fair enough. If I ever need a good cry, a bottle of wine unclogs my emotions every time." She sits on the corner of my bed. "Do you think that's what your engagement party will look like when Jackson proposes? If so, can I DJ? Because the guy from last night committed crimes against music." Her words help me finally realize what felt so wrong with last night. It wasn't really *my* party. It was *our* party. The thought of repeating the event if Jackson did ever propose is unpleasant.

"Absolutely."

18
Saturday
Now

After nearly a week, my calves don't scream in protest as I propel myself forward on the sand. The soles of my feet have thickened slightly, so I don't wince every time I accidentally step on a bit of broken shell. I don't feel like I'm trying to race the feelings of longing that have made the entire trip foggy. Today, I'm running on *my* beach, taking in the memories as I pass them.

I head upstairs to shower when I get back. Everyone else is packing supplies for a day on the boat.

Amber pops her head into Jess's and my room, "Last call for the boat."

"I promise you will all be much happier if I don't join." I have my motion sickness medication, but nothing short of sedating me will make the boat ride enjoyable. "Just promise not to get lost at sea. I would be embarrassed to have to drive the van back to campus all by myself."

"We'll do our best. See you in a couple of hours."

I still plan to enjoy the weather, so I throw on a swimsuit and my Portland hoodie.

Someone knocks on the deck railing steps below like it's a doorway. I see the familiar messy hair and amber eyes. My stomach flips.

"Can I come up?" Bennett calls out. We haven't talked since yesterday.

"Sure." I set the book down and sit up, making space on the bench next to me. Instead of claiming the spot, he sits on a chair nearby.

"They said you were staying behind."

"As you know, I have a rough track record on the water. I didn't think I needed to ruin anyone's lunch by making them hear me heave over the side all day." He winces at my words, recalling my one and only boat ride.

"I was in town helping my mom with some stuff. I wasn't sure how long it would take, so I told them to take off without me." He's so casual, slipping into what we had been like before. I'm not ready to move past all of our unsaid words. We have switched places. He's running while I'm finally willing to stand my ground.

"I was happy to see that you got law school. I saw when you got accepted." It's out of my mouth before I can stop it. I need him to know that I didn't stop caring all that time. He didn't disappear the moment I stopped replying to texts.

"I know," he says, a grin on his face.

"Excuse me?"

He laughs, "You can tell when someone looks at your LinkedIn profile. I stalked you a little too. I'd sometimes take my friends' phones and check what you'd been up to. Well, until last year when you made all your accounts private."

"You're kidding me." I'm mortified thinking of all the people I lowkey stalked because they had no other form of social media. It isn't a small number of people either.

"I dropped my phone when I saw the notification. Still haven't gotten the screen fixed." He holds up his phone to show me the evidence.

"I was really happy for you." I exhale before I continue, "It was surreal to see you doing everything you had dreamed of. It seemed so perfect. It's selfish, but knowing you could do it without me hurt. That you were fine, and I was just treading water, going nowhere."

"I was never fine." He pauses, "I barely got through the semester after you left. I was planning on finding an internship that year, but I couldn't find the energy to start any applications. So, I came back here to help my mom out with the shop. I think part of me hoped you'd change your mind and show up." I had wanted us both to be free of each other.

I get out of my seat to face him properly. "I'm sorry. I never wanted that for you. I never even dreamed up a life where you weren't the most loved, happy person in the room. If I could take all that away from you, I would in an instant. I was a coward and didn't know how to love you the way you deserved."

"Then take it all away, Emma."

One moment I'm standing in front of him. The next, he's pulled me on his lap. His eyes darken. I blink, and his lips are on mine.

It's not last night's kiss full of intense promises and questions. No, we are crashing into each other, finally free from the force that has kept us apart. All of our walls our finally down.

All the pent up emotions pouring out with each touch. Oh, how I want to explore every inch of him, this new Bennett that I haven't had the chance to fully appreciate yet. But we're still the same kids that were desperate for any touch.

A shiver runs through me as his hand skims my stomach, fingers brushing against the edge of my swim top under the hoodie.

"I love how you look in this top. You look the same as the last time you were mine."

"I was never not yours."

"Is this ok? Do you want this?" He pulls away, breathless.

"Yes, this is perfect." How could I want anything else? There is nothing else out there for me. I want more of him, all of him. My mouth returns to his, my fingers caught in his hair. I shift my hips, feeling heat building in me.

"Emma, any more of this, and we'll give the neighbors a show. And seeing how my family is the neighbors-" I don't let him finish, getting off of his lap only to pull him into the house. We don't make it far inside, falling together on the couch. We lose my hoodie in the transition. His hips grind into mine, only adding to my growing need.

"Condom." I trust him and my birth control, but I hadn't gotten tested after learning of Jackson's extracurricular activities.

"Shit, I don't have one." He begins to pull back.

"Jess packed a mega box for the trip. I doubt she'll miss one." I can't run up the stairs fast enough. Once I climb down, prize in hand, I find him at the bottom of the stairs. I waste no time reclaiming his lips.

We move until my back is pressed against the wall. I try to unbutton his shorts, but he grips my wrist, pinning my arm to the wall.

"I'm taking my time with this. I've been thinking about this for the last four years, and I intend to reacquaint myself with every part of you." He starts trailing scorching kisses down my neck. "I need to burn this in my memory just in case it takes another four years to see you like this again." His hand slides into my swim bottoms. I suck in a breath.

"Bennett. Fuck." I only can come up with fragmented words as his fingers work in and out of me. He has me buzzing, hitting all of the right places.

"I'm working on that, be patient." His words brush against the shell of my ear. He uses his other hand to undo the flimsy ties of my top. His mouth covers my now exposed skin.

"Please." I'm so close, but he stops.

"Not yet. I want the first time you come to be with me inside you." I love this new, commanding part of him. All I can do is blink up at him, my mind blank, needing more. I pull at the hem of his shirt. I had seen him on the beach plenty of times this week, but now I can take in all of him, appreciating him like the work of art he is. He tenses as I run my fingers over him, tracing the ink on the left side of his chest. The tattoo is a minimalist rendering of a wave.

The ocean was always his first love. I had once promised myself I would be the only other love to follow.

I lower his shorts and take him in my hand, moving just as slowly and intentionally as he had for me.

"Emma," he murmurs like my name is the last word in existence. I savor the sound of my name on his tongue, where it belongs.

"Say my name like that again."

"Emma." He lifts me by my waist onto the counter. "Fuck patience. I need you." The feeling of the marble is like ice against my hot skin. I hear the tear of the condom wrapper; moments later, he is between my legs moving into me. I can't contain the sounds that escape at the first feeling of him. My hands are lost in his hair, and my legs are hooked around him.

He braces against me with one hand while the other lightly brushes my breasts and stomach in circles that make my insides flutter. He moves lower, pressing into my bundle of nerves as he continues to thrust inside of me. My eyes flutter closed, taking in all of the sensations.

"Look at me." When I do, I drown in his eyes, intoxicated by having him in the way I had pretended not to crave. That look is my undoing. It isn't long before he follows me over the edge.

We stay there, taking in all that we are now. Letting the years between us fade away.

"We are so much better at that now." His voice cuts through the crackling air. He is right. I don't know if I should personally mail thank you letters to all of the people he's slept with or make sure their numbers are deleted from his phone.

"We really did that."

"I'm far from done. I have four years to make up for and other men to erase from your memory." He sinks lower until his face is pressed between my thighs. I don't stifle the moans that escape me.

Our bodies remember all of the places we've done this before. We never shook the habit of each other, and this is proof.

Hours later, sheets are tangled around us, and we've made a noticeable dent in Jess's supply of condoms. His fingers are dancing up and down my arms, nose nuzzling my neck.

"Is it fucked up that I was happy that you ran away that first day? I had thought all this time you didn't care as much as I did. I was relieved to see you hurting just a little bit." He asks.

"It is, but I get it. I tried so hard not to think about you, but when I did, I could only picture that you were happier. That you were with someone that made you so happy that you forgot about me. It made me feel fucking terrible that I wanted you to keep needing me after everything that happened."

"We can be terrible together now."

"What if we choose to be happy instead?"

"That sounds like a much better option." I feel the smile on his lips as they press against mine. I am fully and completely satiated off him. I don't want to leave tomorrow.

"I have an idea. Can you ask your parents if they want to come over for dinner tonight? It feels wrong not to eat with them at least once."

"I feel like I should be offended that we just had the best sex of our lives, and you're thinking about dinner with my parents. Let me check." He types for a second on his phone, and it almost immediately lights up with a response. "So, the answer is yes and no. Yes, they would love to have dinner. No, there is absolutely no way they will have it anywhere else but at our place." I secretly hoped that's what she would say. Diane always hated how boring this place was, and I couldn't picture her being here for an entire evening.

We let everyone know about the dinner plans when they get back. Bennett is still here, and no one is subtle about the looks that they give us.

Before heading to dinner, I call my uncle about my decision. The next few months start to look less bleak.

The smell of freshly baked cheese rolls and pasta hit us before we even reach the first step. My stomach rumbles thinking of all the years I had deprived myself of Diane's baking and Richard's cooking.

When my parents visited Haven during my sophomore year, I had been more concerned with how soon I could get them to leave than whether they would get along with my friends. Now a wash of nerves runs through me as we reach the deck covered in its strings of sparkling lights.

Once again, I imagine what it would have been like if Bennett and I had been together all this time. Would I have brought my friends here sooner? I would have loved to share more memories of this place with them. A fist squeezes my heart, thinking of what could have been.

No, because if Bennett and I had followed through on our plans, I wouldn't have met them. I wouldn't know that when Libby laughs, the occasional snort slips out or that Caleb can point out any constellation in the sky. It was all worth it, no matter how terrible.

This time when my worlds collide, it works. Caleb and Tanner riff off each other like they've been friends for years.

Libby and Diane discuss which websites have the best daily horoscopes and which are hoaxes. Richard challenges Josh to an arm wrestling contest, and we all cheer as they draw it out longer than needed, with Richard winning. My friends give the Sorensons a run for their money with the insults and threats they make during cards.

The best part of it is that they're all mine.

We make our way inside after eating on the deck. Amber and Libby are helping Diane clean up the kitchen. All eight of us would be in there if we weren't shoved out. It's the same house, but the small things have shifted. There are more pictures and collections of shells. The years I have been absent are marked by the accumulation of stuff.

"Who's this?" I pick up a picture of Jones and an elegant woman on vacation somewhere tropical.

"That's his wife," Bennett tells me. I look more intently.

"Wife. Damn. I didn't think he had it in him." The Jones I knew wasn't the type who knew what he wanted next month. Him committing to forever with someone was a beautiful impossibility.

"He's settled down the last few years. Lives in Boston, and she teaches third grade. The wedding was last summer. Mom said she sent an invite to your home address. Sounds like you never got it." I remember a text from Diane asking for an address, but like all the other messages from her, I never responded. What would I have done if I had gotten it? I can't picture Jackson as my plus-one mingling with the

Sorensons and all their craziness. Who would I have been, tucked in at his side? Definitely not the Emma that they intended to invite. Maybe not receiving it was a good thing.

My mind drifts to my mother. She's the only one who would intentionally make certain that I never received it. Her intent wouldn't have been to keep me from reliving the pain. She likely just wanted to keep me away from risking my future with Jackson.

The ever growing ache makes itself known again. I hate not knowing this earlier. Things change, but I wasn't there to change with them. I'm reminded that only being here for a few days doesn't make up for lost years. New discoveries keep piling up.

The night ends as everyone says their goodbyes and a few tears are shed over new friendships. My friends, head to bed or start packing for tomorrow's drive. I'm sitting on the edge of the deck with Bennett, sipping wine out of plastic cups.

"I feel like I've missed so much. There are so many things I don't know about you," I say.

"Then ask."

"I don't know where to start."

"Let's make it a game. You can only ask three questions and then, next time, three more. This way, I can keep some of the new mysterious parts of me captive until I get to see you again."

"Have you really never taken anyone else back here?" I can feel the hope in my voice.

"Only once. Sophomore year of college, I was dating this guy, and I brought him back for winter break. But I realized after seeing him with my family he just didn't fit. Like trying to shove a puzzle piece into a spot that looks like it should work, but the shape isn't quite right, and the colors don't add up. We broke up after we drove back to campus."

"Why didn't you ever tell me you were bi?"

"I didn't really figure out that part of myself until college. I think a big part was that I couldn't picture myself with anyone else but you for the longest time." I lean into him, needing to absorb his warmth against the light chill. "You have one more question, Danes."

"Will you come to my graduation?"

"I don't think that question really fits the game." But to me, it does. Because what I'm really asking is *Will you be a part of my real life? The life we promised each other so long ago.* "But yes, I can't think of any place I'd rather be." He kisses my forehead.

I don't know how long we stay out there. But eventually, my fingers become stiff in the cold night air, and I force myself to leave, knowing I have to sleep if I'm going to help clean the house in the morning.

19
Sunday
Now

It's time to leave again. This time I leave with a promise to return. Diane made me sit down with her and pick two weekends to fly back this year.

I was ready to say goodbye to this house seven days ago. Hell, I even considered burning it down, as Bennett requested. I'm happy we made memories in it this week to replace the hollowness it once held. Though I'm not sure if I'll ever be ready to say goodbye to Harriettesville again, my time in this house is over. Now whenever I come back, I'll just be one door over in a perfect pink home.

We did some reversible damage throughout the week that draws out the cleaning. After a thorough sweep and vacuum, we collected enough sand to make our own beach. Libby and Amber had been religious about collecting empty bottles and cans for recycling. I'm about the size of the clinking bag I heave into the bin.

I'm doing one more sweep of the master to make sure that we didn't leave anything behind when I finally get the nerve to return my mother's calls. She picks up on the second ring.

"Did you call Jackson?" I don't care what she's been wanting to talk about.

"Emma, it's customary to say hello when calling someone." That never seemed to apply whenever she ambushed me with calls. She's stalling, not ready for me to confront her.

"Don't change the subject. He told me already."

"So?"

"So what?"

"So, what should I tell your father about graduation? We still need to make plans." Is she fucking joking? Did she really think she could fix Jackson and my relationship with a manipulative phone call?

"Mom, let me make something perfectly clear. Whatever delusional reality Dad and your relationship is in doesn't work for me. If you don't think I deserve more than Jackson, I'm asking you to keep your thoughts on my dating life to yourself."

"Emma Claire!" She shouts. It's euphoric getting this big of a reaction out of her. The feeling pushes me to continue.

"Also, any chance you threw away a wedding invitation addressed to me last year?"

"I didn't think you talked to those people anymore. I didn't want to hurt you by sending it along." It's a valid excuse. I'm still not sure how I would have reacted if I picked it out of the mail.

"Well, you'll be happy to hear Bennett and I made up. In fact, he'll be at my graduation, so that's something you and Dad can plan on since you're so concerned about it. Also, I gave Uncle Henry a call about his offer."

"I'll make arrangements to include them then. What did you tell him? Since you're not going to New York with Jackson, I assume you chose D.C.?" I can hear that she's regained her composure, but there is still tension in her words.

"I'm taking the offer in Chicago. Bennett's going to law school there. I think being nearby will really help us reconnect." I feel a certain type of pleasure, twisting her carefully laid plans into something I want. Not only will I be in the same city as Bennett it's also the furthest distance from D.C. of any of the offices.

"That's great to hear." My shoulders relax as she doesn't fight me on the compromise. I take the job she's been bugging me about, and I don't catch shit for being back with Bennett.

"We're about to hit the road. I'll talk to you later," I add in a casual tone as if I didn't just tell my mother I finally wrestled control of my life out of her hands. It feels appropriate that this conversation took place in the same room where she lectured me about proper relationships and planning for a certain type of life.

Though we didn't do much shopping this week, we have to play Tetris to make everything fit. Just as we shove Libby's sticker covered suitcase into position, I start to think I'm missing something.

"I'll be right back." I've almost forgotten something essential. The old habit of forcibly not thinking of the Sorensons around my friends is still a little too strong this early in the morning.

I run next door as fast as I can manage.

I open the front door without a second thought and pray that the guys aren't off on some adventure this morning. I see their shoes by the entrance, but that doesn't mean much on the beach.

"Upstairs," Tanner says through a mouth full of cereal.

"Thanks."

He garbles something like, "No problem," as I bolt up the stairs.

Bennett's door is slightly ajar, with light music trickling out. I push it open to find the guys surrounded by thick law textbooks and loose pages of cramped handwritten notes.

Jordan is on his stomach, kicking his feet like they pose girls in 90s shows getting a call. He's mouthing things, but his eyes look glazed over. Theo has so many pieces of paper around him I'm not sure where the notes end and his legs start. Bennett is zoned in at his desk, tapping his foot to the music.

"Hey." I attempt to sound casual and not like I'm dying for air. They were so tuned into their work that they didn't notice I was standing there. "Umm, we're about to head out, and I just wanted to say goodbye."

Everyone had technically said goodbye last night.

"I think I need a refill." Theo holds up his mug. When Jordan doesn't move, Bennett crumples a piece of paper and throws it at his friend.

"Oh, me too." Jordan rolls to his feet, leaving me and Bennett alone in his room.

Nothing has changed beyond the addition of a few more pictures. I pick up the frame of one that shows his college graduation, an event I had hoped to be a part of. I know that I'll be at the next one no matter what happens. I'm just happy I get a redo.

As I look, he stands up and wraps his arms around me. I feel at home in his arms. Little satisfying feelings run through me as his fingers dance across my skin, in rhythm with whatever he's listening to. I just hope he's having the same thoughts I am.

I set down the picture, surprised to see what it was next to.

"You kept it." I look so young and happy next to Richard's vinyl collection.

"I told you I never let you go. I will admit that I tried to throw it away once after drinking with Tanner, but it was right back on the desk the next day," he says. God, I love Diane.

I turn in his arms to face him, pulling his face to mine. I draw out our kiss. This last kiss will have to sustain me until the next time I see him. He lifts me onto his desk, and I wrap my legs around his waist. We stay like that until someone clears their throat.

"Please tell me you guys didn't do anything to desecrate my notes. I really don't want to have to throw them away." Jordan is in the doorway, holding a fresh cup. "Emma, there is an angry mob outside looking for you. They said something about storming the house if you don't get down there soon."

"Fine. If you can't hold them off any longer." I slide down as Bennett releases his hold.

I want to tell him I love him. But I wasn't lying when I said I wanted to ease into this. I'll love him in secret for a while longer. Well not secret because we've already all but said it outright.

I'm exiled to the cramped back corner of the van for the travel delay I caused. Tucked away, I still get to watch the landscape in the way I used to appreciate it. The scent of the salt air dissipates as we drive through trees back toward Haven.

A few hours into the drive, we're still not sick of each other and are talking about anything that comes to mind.

"If you could redo life over again, what would you change?" Amber asks.

"How existential of you. Dr. Mottz would be proud." Caleb is right; the Creative Thinking professor would be ecstatic to hear the words coming out of Amber's mouth.

"I take it back then."

"Nope. I like the question. I think I wouldn't go to school at all. I would become a raft guide, and when starting getting too old, I'd start a farm," Libby starts us off.

"I would open a little beach town boutique," Jess says, still holding on to this newly formed dream.

Caleb says he would stay on the farm with his family and sleep under the stars as often as possible. Amber tells us about how she thought it would always be fun to be a professor, but for a real subject, of course. Instead of football, Josh says he would have pursued hockey.

"I don't think I'd change anything," I add. If Amber had asked this a week ago, I would have had a list of regrets ready to recite. Now it feels like everything has fallen into place.

"That's not the question. You have to have something you'd change," Amber says.

"Fine, I would have never dated that shit dick Jackson and I would have brought you all here much sooner. I don't care if, in this alternate universe, we never go to college together. I would hunt each of you down and bring you with me."

Jackson was an unfortunate necessity in drawing me back to this place. I think if it hadn't been now, it would have been later. The beach and my Sorensons would have brought me back one way or another.

"Amen. That man never deserved to be in your life." Jess raises her iced coffee in a cheers.

"But we can all agree that the new one has promise. Or is he considered the old one? Either way, I hope he sticks."

"Me too. Besides, who else's beach house would we use next time we're all together?" I take it all in.

How did I get so lucky to be surrounded by so many people who are so perfect for me?

20

Spring
Two months later

Libby squeezes my hand before we take the stage. The others are already on the other side, looping back to their seats. Our crimson graduation robes billow around us as we take the last steps.

As I shake the administrators' hands, I pause momentarily and look out to the crowd. There is a small section of people cheering for me. I had to email the graduation coordinator begging for the four extra tickets, but the groveling was absolutely worth it to have the Sorensons here.

They have a sign with a blown up picture of my face and the words '#1 fans of Emma Danes' written in what is unmistakably Tanner's handwriting. Next to them are my parents and Corrina. Rigid, but still proud to see me make this milestone. Together the group comprises my past and my future.

When I told Bennett I accepted the marketing position in Chicago, we agreed not to move in with each other for at least the first year. He had been right all those years ago- we had created a perfect bubble, and now we needed to see how this worked in the real world. He even offered to fake meet me for the first time at a café and make me fall in love with him all over again.

"If you mess this up again, I'm disowning you and adopting her as my youngest child," Diane said when we told her the plan last month. I had gone back to Harriettesville for a weekend to help celebrate Bennett finishing his first year of law school.

My friends and I head outside, mingling and trying to find our family members.

"I think your sister just threatened to ruin my career if I ever break your heart. I really think she means it, too," Bennett says in awe. Corrina absolutely means it.

"You should see what she did to her last boyfriend." She dropped the guy's ride share passenger ratings so low that he could only use the subway or get a proper taxi. I laugh, but he's right. Over the years, Corrina has grown more protective.

Bennett landed a law internship in D.C. for the summer, which gives me an excuse to spend one last summer at home.

My parents are more willing to accept our relationship now that they see that Bennett has a future they approve of. I did have to save him from Dad's lecture about environmental law and policy being a terrible focus to go into.

After the ceremony, we head to Zenith, where my parents have set up a party. It's eerily similar to my 21st. The main difference is there's no dance floor or DJ. As promised, I let Libby make a playlist.

"Are you ready to go?" Bennett whispers into my ear.

"You want me to dip out on my own party?"

"Name one of those ten people, and we'll stay." He points to a group of people in their forties. No, he wins on this one. I can't pick out a face, not to mention a name.

"Fine, but you get the first shift driving tomorrow."

"I wouldn't have it any other way."

"Let's say goodbye to everyone first. We need to let them know they are free to escape." My friends have been in their own corner while I made the rounds with Bennett.

Josh had nearly tackled him when Bennett got in from his flight a few days ago. I learned that he has to take sleeping pills because he doesn't do well on flights. I've started to collect a series of observations from real world Bennett. He can only fall asleep on the right side of the bed, and if he has a chance, he brushes his teeth after every meal.

He flew out so he can help me drive the moving van from Virginia to Chicago. After we stow the boxes in his apartment, we're going on a road trip to the handful of National Parks in the Midwest before we head to D.C. I want to go to Chicago first for selfish reasons. Mostly because I want to see the city he's been living in, but also because it means I don't have to store my stuff in D.C. for the summer.

The next morning, I roll over and kiss him on the nose. The brush of my lips causes his eyes to flutter open.

"Are you ready?" I ask.

"Ready to get on the road or ready to start the rest of our lives?" his voice is rough with the remnants of sleep.

"Both."

"I've never had a doubt about forever. But I can't say the same about the truck."

21
Epilogue

The coffee shop door swings open, letting in a rush of bone-chilling air. Chicago winter has forced me to bundle up in thick layers, which take forever to put on every morning. It's been two years since I moved to the Windy City, and I'm still not used to it.

I look up to see a man walk in; he wears a thick sweater under a long coat. The cold makes his cheeks and nose rosy.

I look back down at my latte, not wanting to be caught staring. Even from that one glimpse, I can tell that though the city looks good on him, he was born to be at the beach. His sandy waves stick up haphazardly from being out in the wind, and even though it's winter, he has the last hint of a lingering tan. I can't help but pay attention as he orders the same drink I did. He's magnetic. His voice flows to me through the bustle of the other people in the coffee shop. It's rough but inviting, the sound of someone always on the verge of laughter.

"Is this seat taken?" His hand rests on the back of the chair across from me.

"No, it's all yours." I look up, my gaze catching the heat in his eyes. They have the warm glow of a flickering fire. Instead of taking the chair and moving it to an empty space, like a normal person would, he sits at my table. He sets his mug down next to mine. As he settles into his chair, our knees brush, sending a shock of electricity through me.

"Let me guess, honey, cinnamon latte?" He smiles, not registering the effect he has on me.

"Yeah, but in the summer, I add lavender in it too," I say. But those are always iced, of course.

"Me too. What a coincidence." His mouth quirks up into a smirk as he takes a sip. When he lowers the mug, a streak of foam is left on his upper lip.

"Umm, you have a bit of." I gesture to my own lip.

"You're not going to get it for me?"

"You have to take me on a date before I get anywhere near your mouth." At my response, his tongue flicks out to catch the smudge of foam. My eyes are fixed on his lips and the little pale scar near his cupid's bow.

"That can be arranged. I'm thinking drinks."

"With karaoke."

"Obviously. What's a better way to get to know someone than their taste in pop ballads?"

"On second thought." I feign getting up to leave.

"I'll make it worth your while." His eyes glitter playfully.

"Promise." I hold out my pinkie.

"You want to pinkie promise right now?" He asks.

"Haven't you heard? Pinkie promises are totally hardcore."

"Whoever told you that must be pretty wise." He wraps his finger around mine.

"He only thinks he is."

"We're pretty good at this meet cute thing, aren't we?" Bennett shatters the illusion. He didn't even last ten minutes. It's five minutes longer than the last time he tried and seven minutes longer than the time before that.

"We were until you broke character just now. You're supposed to not know me."

"Pretending to not know you is one of the hardest things in the world. As someone who's tried a couple of times, I don't recommend it." He picks up my hand and presses it to his lips. Lips that no longer taste of the ocean. In the winter, he tastes of peppermints and cinnamon from the candies he always has in his pockets.

"I still want karaoke."

"Anything. Everything. I'll meet you again in every coffee shop in the world and take you to every shitty karaoke bar. You promised all your summers, and I plan to collect, Emma Claire Sorenson."

Acknowledgements

It's not hard to know where to start. There is one person who started this process. One day I was brave enough to show the start of a story to my roommate, not this story. Stef told me it could be something, and I believed her. I'm so happy I did. After, she designed this cover, helped with edits, and so much more. She always listened, even when I spoiled the plot.

Stella, my fellow daydreamer. I know I can always obsess over summer boys with her. There are so many lines that made me feel like kicking my feet and giggling; they're all for her.

Of course, there is everyone at Ernest & Hadley Books. Without them, I wouldn't be reading or writing again.

And last, my family for having books. Growing up in a house that listened to more books than music formed me in ways I can't adequately describe.

Made in the USA
Columbia, SC
15 August 2023